"We just got married and already we have a son?"

Travis asked Katie with a nervous laugh. "Did I know about this?"

Katie swallowed hard before nodding. She'd become so engrossed in making Travis understand about her nephew's custody hearing that telling a lie—even in a just cause and after she'd told so many tonight—suddenly didn't feel right.

"Katie..." He sounded oddly tentative. "Did we get married just for this hearing?"

"I'd never marry for that reason," she said.

"I'm glad to hear that." Travis lifted his hand to her cheek, then let his fingers trail down her neck. She didn't flinch, enjoying the sensation and wanting more.

How was that possible? How could she enjoy the touch of a man who worked for her parents, a man who would ruin everything when he regained his memory?

Dear Reader,

What makes a man a Fabulous Father? For me, he's the man who married my single mother when she had three little kids (who all needed braces) and raised us as his own. And, to celebrate an upcoming anniversary of the Romance line's FABULOUS FATHERS series, I'd like to know *your* thoughts on what makes a man a Fabulous Father. Send me a brief (50 words) note with your name, city and state, giving me permission to publish all or portions of your note, and you just might see it printed on a special page.

Blessed with a baby—and a second chance at marriage—this month's FABULOUS FATHER also has to become a fabulous husband to his estranged wife in *Introducing Daddy* by Alaina Hawthorne.

"Will you marry me, in name only?" That's a woman's desperate question to the last of THE BEST MEN, Karen Rose Smith's miniseries, in *A Groom and a Promise.*

He drops her like a hot potato, then comes back with babies and wants her to be his nanny! Or so he says...in *Babies and a Blue-Eyed Man* by Myrna Mackenzie.

When a man has no memory and a woman needs an instant husband, she tells him a little white lie and presto! in *My Favorite Husband* by Sally Carleen.

She's a waitress who needs etiquette lessons in becoming a lady; he's a millionaire who likes her just the way she is in *Wife in Training* by Susan Meier.

Finally, Robin Wells is one of Silhouette's WOMEN TO WATCH—a new author debuting in the Romance line with *The Wedding Kiss.*

I hope you enjoy all our books this month—and every month!

Regards,

Melissa Senate,
Senior Editor

MY FAVORITE HUSBAND

Sally Carleen

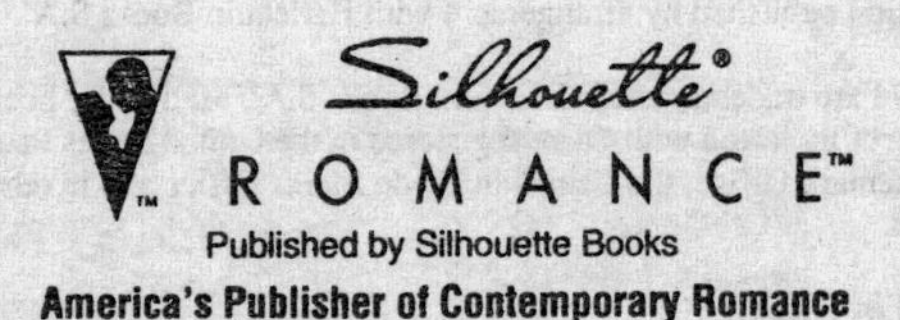

Published by Silhouette Books
America's Publisher of Contemporary Romance

To Teri Frailey and to John Dunn, whoever he may be

ISBN 0-373-19183-9

MY FAVORITE HUSBAND

This edition published by arrangement with Harlequin Books S.A.

Printed in U.S.A.

Books by Sally Carleen

Silhouette Romance

An Improbable Wife #1101
Cody's Christmas Wish #1124
My Favorite Husband #1183

Silhouette Shadows

Shaded Leaves of Destiny #46

SALLY CARLEEN

For as long as she can remember, Sally planned to be a writer when she grew up. Finally, one day, after more years than she cares to admit, she realized she was as grown up as she was likely to become, and began to write romance novels. In the years prior to her epiphany, Sally supported her writing habit by working as a legal secretary, a real estate agent, a legal assistant, a leasing agent, an executive secretary and in various other occupations.

She now writes full-time, and looks upon her previous careers as research and/or torture. A native of McAlester, Oklahoma, and naturalized citizen of Dallas, Texas, Sally now lives in Lee's Summit, Missouri, with her husband, Max, their very large cat, Leo, and a very small dog, Cricket. Her interests, besides writing, are chocolate and Classic Coke.

Readers can write to Sally at P.O. Box 6614, Lee's Summit, MO 64086.

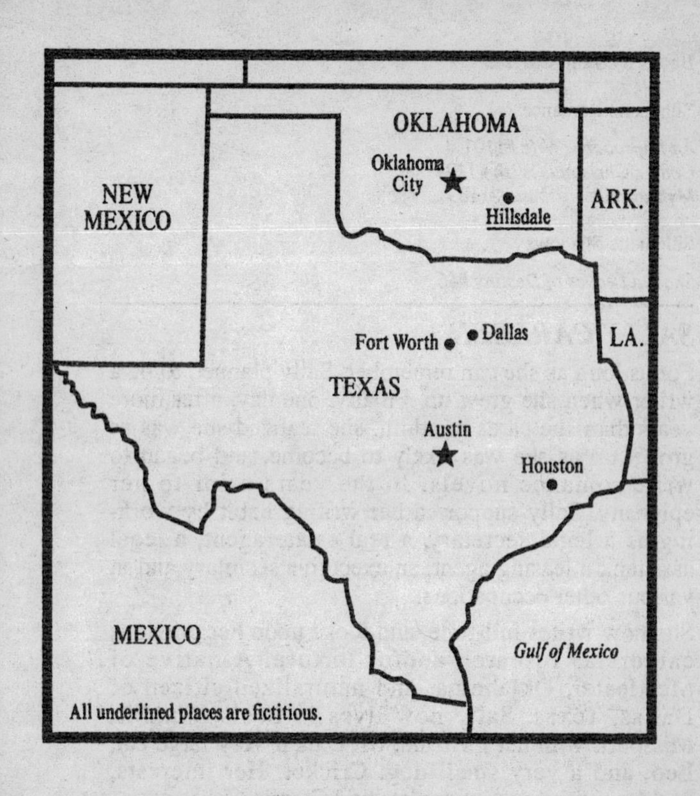
OKLAHOMA
Oklahoma City
Hillsdale
ARK.
NEW MEXICO
Fort Worth
Dallas
LA.
TEXAS
Austin
Houston
MEXICO
Gulf of Mexico
All underlined places are fictitious.

Chapter One

"Oh, no!" In the stillness of the Dallas summer night, Katie Logan's exclamation carried quite clearly through the open window to where Travis Rider crouched in the overgrown shrubbery. "John, this is terrible. Isn't there any way you can get the next two days off?"

"I'm sorry, Katie, but you know how strict the hospital is about these schedules. I'd do it for you if I could."

"I know you would. I just don't have a clue what to do now. The custody hearing starts tomorrow. I've already told the social worker we're married. How am I ever going to find somebody to be my husband by then?"

In spite of his cynical nature, Travis couldn't suppress a brief flash of disappointment at those words. Katie Logan was bright, charming and witty, not to mention that she had long, slinky legs, a nicely rounded rear that matched her higher endowments and big blue eyes in the face of an angel. He hadn't wanted to believe she was completely irresponsible, a total flake, but this conversation destroyed any vestige of doubt.

Holding the directional microphone of his tape recorder as close as possible to the open window, he shifted from his uncomfortable position and eased another couple of inches through the scratchy but concealing foliage. After years of detective work, Travis had developed an almost photographic memory for conversations, but it never hurt to have a backup recording, especially of something as important as this dialogue.

"Katie, I'm sorry," the would-be husband said. "I was all ready to go when I got the new schedule. My bags are packed and in the car. I tried every way I could to get out of it, but I'm just an intern. I don't have much say in scheduling."

"Didn't you tell them how important this is?"

She sounded devastated. If Travis hadn't known better, he could almost feel sorry for her. But he did know better. He knew Katie's type.

"What was I going to tell them? That I had to have the next couple of days off so I could pretend to be your husband? That'd look real good on my record."

Travis smiled grimly into the darkness. This would be just the evidence his clients needed to insure that Katie didn't get custody of her eight-year-old nephew. He hadn't been overly impressed with the Logans when he'd talked to them on the phone, but thank goodness he'd taken the job anyway. Thank goodness he'd kept after Katie until he uncovered the truth. He knew he shouldn't get personally involved in his work, but in this instance, it was impossible not to.

Katie Logan had no business raising her nephew... no more than his own equally irresponsible mother had raising him. From the age of six, when his parents were divorced, he had gone through five stepfathers and probably twenty schools across the country. If he could stop that from happening to another child, then his own experience would have been worth it.

Travis realized he was gritting his teeth...and not listening closely to the conversation inside the house. He consciously loosened his jaw and focused on what Katie's friend was saying.

"It'll be all right. Just show them the marriage license. It looks like the real thing. How can they doubt you? Besides, you've shown your stability with this house and your job, and the caseworker told you her report would be favorable. You have nothing to worry about. You're a terrific person. I can't imagine why your parents are trying to do this."

As Travis scanned the scene inside the house, he realized he could no longer see Katie. She must be there, however, since her friend continued to talk and gesticulate—nervously and nonstop—and Travis was getting every word of it on the tape recorder in his hand as well as the one in his head.

Though the late May night was warm, especially since he was wearing a leather jacket for protection against the bushes, an inexplicable chill darted down his spine, a warning that all wasn't right. He shook off the sensation. Things couldn't possibly be any more right.

Before this night was over, he'd have all the evidence the Logans would need to get custody of their grandson. Maybe they weren't bubbling and effusive, but they'd give the boy a good, stable home. Tomorrow he'd file his report and make plans to testify at the hearing, if necessary. Katie Logan would never be able to ruin her nephew's childhood the way his mother had ruined his.

While John kept talking as though she were still in the room, Katie took her iron skillet from the top of the stove and crept stealthily out the back door. During the year she'd spent assisting a study group in the Amazon rain forest, she'd learned to listen and observe. For the past couple of weeks she'd had the eerie feeling she was being followed, though until tonight she'd never seen any hard evidence. But now she was pretty sure some pervert was hiding in the shrubbery outside her living room window.

Moving as quietly as possible, she circled around behind the bushes. Her heart rate went up dramatically as she saw the crouching figure. Knowing somebody was out there was one thing; actually *seeing* that somebody was quite another.

She stood paralyzed, rooted to the spot by shock, not daring to breathe lest the person turn and see her. The cool handle of the skillet suddenly burned her fingers, and she could feel the perspiration making it slippery. This time her impetuosity had gotten her into a real jam. Whatever had possessed her to come outside alone in the first place?

Then she noticed a hand extending from the shrubbery toward the window, a hand holding a gun pointed at John. Adrenaline surged through her, fear and anger releasing her from shock, sending her forward in a mad rush, her iron skillet swinging wildly.

The prowler turned toward her, eyes widening in surprise, just as her weapon connected with the side of his head. His eyes closed, and with a groan, he crumpled to the ground.

Katie dropped her skillet in horror and sank to the ground beside the prowler.

"Katie!" John called from the window. "What's going on? Are you all right?"

"No! Oh, John, I just killed a man! Call an ambulance! Come do CPR!"

She lifted the man's wrist and felt for a pulse, but all she could feel was her own heart pounding.

The front door slammed, and John ran up beside her.

"He had a gun," she said. "He was going to shoot you." Then she groaned more loudly and more painfully than the man had when she'd whacked him. "This isn't going to look so good at the custody hearing, is it? Being a murderer probably won't help establish my stability."

Nathan needed her to look stable. Her nephew was counting on her. If she let him down, he'd have to live with her father. She shivered. No, that was unthinkable. She wouldn't let him down in spite of this sudden catastrophe. Somehow she'd save him.

John knelt beside the man and pressed his fingers to his neck. "You didn't kill him. He's still very much alive. A good strong heartbeat. Probably works out regularly. Where'd you hit him?"

"On the left side, kind of in front, I think. I don't know. It happened so fast. I was aiming for the back of his head, and he turned around."

John pushed the man's hair off his face, then ran his fingers over the scalp. "I can't tell for sure in the dark, but I don't think you did much damage. I can't feel any bleeding. He should be coming around any minute. You go call the police while I stay here and watch him."

Katie closed her eyes for a second, daring to take a deep breath of relief. When she'd left home ten years ago, her stated goal in life had been to experience everything at least once, but that *everything* hadn't included murder. She started to get up and follow John's directions, then stopped and knelt back down.

"What's this?" A small tape recorder lay beside the man. "The pervert was going to record your murder!" She snatched up the machine and stood. A wire with a small cylindrical object on the end dangled from it.

John looked up at her uncertainly. "A murderer with a tape recorder? Katie, I don't see a gun. Are you sure he had one? Are you sure you didn't maybe see that microphone?"

Katie reeled up the microphone and studied it closely. "No," she said quietly, "I guess I'm not sure. In the dark, I could've been mistaken. He could've been holding this thing. Even so, he had no business prowling around my house and recording our conversation. I'm going to call the police."

But she didn't move. The temperature seemed to rise ten degrees. The air pressed heavily against her chest, making it hard to breathe. In the quiet night—far, far away, it seemed, in a world where normal people lived—a dog barked.

"Prowlers don't usually have tape recorders, do they?" she said after a long moment.

"How would I know? I haven't had much experience with prowlers. I once took a bullet out of one in ER, but that's about the extent of my knowledge."

Katie turned the recorder over, studying it as closely as possible in the faint light from the living room window and from the street lamp. Oddly, in the summer heat the object felt cold. "This thing's got some kind of a plate on it, maybe a nameplate, but I can't read what it says. Would a prowler put his name on his equipment?"

"I don't know. Maybe this guy stole it."

"Maybe." There it was again, that niggling feeling she'd been trying to discount for the past week, that sixth sense that things were out of kilter. A horrible suspicion—a fear greater than when she'd thought herself faced with a man holding a gun—darted around the edges of her thoughts.

Tossing the recorder aside, she once again knelt beside the prone man. "Help me roll him over."

"Are you nuts?" John protested, leaning back on his heels. "We've got to call the police. Knocking him out is one thing, but rolling him around afterward just won't do."

"I need to find his wallet. I've got to know who he is."

"What on earth for? Katie, I've gone along with a couple of your schemes that sounded pretty crazy, including pretending to be your husband, but I draw the line at this. If you're not going to call the police, I will, and I'll leave you alone with this guy who could wake up at any minute."

John started to stand, but Katie grabbed his arm. "Please. Just this one more favor."

He sighed, but he grasped the man's shoulders and heaved. Katie jumped as the man moaned when John eased him up onto his side.

"He's still out," John assured her. "Go on. Do whatever demented thing you think you have to do and get this over with before one of your neighbors sees us and thinks we're all perverts."

With two fingers, Katie reached inside the hip pocket of the man's black jeans and tentatively withdrew his wallet. The soft leather was warm from his body, and she felt as though she were touching him intimately. Swallowing hard, she gathered her courage.

She stood and moved closer to the window to take advantage of the light, then opened the wallet. Her heart plummeted as her blackest fears were confirmed. "He's a private detective," she said, forcing the words from her suddenly dry throat.

"What!"

"My parents must have hired him to spy on me. I knew it! They've been too quiet lately. It's not like them to stop harassing me all of a sudden. For the past week, I've had the feeling that somebody was following me, watching me, and I was right. Damn his sorry, rotten hide!"

She stomped back to where John still knelt beside the man—beside Travis Rider, Private Investigator. Laying the wallet on the ground, she bent over him and steeled herself to touch him again, to reach inside his black leather jacket and search his pockets.

The action stirred the masculine scents of leather and after-shave—pleasant, compelling scents in the midst of an ominous, distasteful situation. A soft

T-shirt stretched over hard, well-developed muscles that threatened to distract her from her quest.

Reaching into an inner jacket pocket, she withdrew a comb, a gold pen and an envelope with a canceled postage stamp in one corner. Even in the near darkness she could make out the bold, stern strokes of her father's handwriting in the address that covered most of the envelope.

With numb fingers, she opened it and extracted a single sheet of paper, a form with TRAVIS RIDER, PRIVATE INVESTIGATOR, in block letters at the top, CONTRACT on the next line and Ralph Logan's imperious signature at the bottom. The printing in between was too small to make out in the dim light, but she didn't need to know the particulars.

This man was helping her parents get custody of her orphaned nephew. This man would doom Nathan to grow up in the repressed, restricted, nightmarish way she'd had to grow up. She considered kicking him, but wasn't sure he'd feel it while he was unconscious. Maybe after he woke up.

John retrieved the tape recorder and stood, offering it to her. "Katie, he probably recorded our conversation. He must know what you were planning to do. Do you want to take the tape and destroy it?"

Katie sagged back down with a muttered curse. "It won't matter. He's bound to have heard it all."

She shoved at the man's shoulder, eliciting another groan, but she didn't care. Let him groan. Let him feel a small portion of the pain his actions would cause.

"Why'd you have to do it? Maybe I haven't had the same job or the same address for twenty years, but I love my nephew. That's more than my parents can say. They'll crush the life out of him the same way they did

Becky and me. Damn you, Travis Rider.'' She shoved again. ''May your wife run off with your best friend and all your hair fall out.''

''Jeez, I can't believe you conked the detective who's out to get you,'' John said. ''That probably won't help your case any.''

''Probably not. Though I can't imagine it could make things any worse.'' She sighed, then cursed again. ''Well, we can't give up. I owe it to my sister. I owe it to Nathan. We have to figure a way out of this.''

''Katie, you're licked. I tried to tell you from the beginning you'd never get away with this. Even if it worked, your parents would get visitation, and they'd find out from Nathan that we weren't really married, then you'd be in a real mess.''

''I told you, Nathan's a cool kid. He'd never tell those people anything. Besides, with the hours you work, even if we were married, I'd never see you.''

''Well, it's a moot point now. You might as well give it up.''

Katie slammed her fists onto her hips. ''No way. I will not let Becky's son be raised by those cold, hard people. Help me get this guy inside the house. Maybe we can talk some sense into him when he comes around. Maybe if he understands the situation, he won't testify against me. Or maybe we can just tie him up and lock him in the closet until after the hearing. You could come over and throw him a raw egg or a mouse now and then. That's what snakes eat, isn't it?''

''If the hospital finds out about this, I'm dead.''

''If this doesn't work, an innocent child is doomed.''

''Have you been reading Charles Dickens again?''

Katie leaned over, picked up the wallet and stuffed it into her own pocket rather than have to touch the detective again, then lifted his legs. "Get his arms," she instructed, "and stop worrying. All you're doing is helping to get this injured man inside where you can examine him in your medical capacity. The rest is entirely on my shoulders. So quit complaining. Where's your sense of honor?" She wasn't sure what type of honor she was challenging him about, but it seemed a good thing to appeal to at the time.

John grabbed Rider's shoulders and lifted.

Travis Rider was tall and heavy. He wasn't fat; Katie suspected the weight was almost all muscle. John had said his heartbeat suggested he worked out regularly, and she'd felt his solid chest. If they couldn't reach him through reason, they had no chance of overpowering him physically. Unless they tied him up before he regained consciousness.

Together she and John dragged him along the rough earth, across the stubbles of grass she hadn't been able to make grow, over to the front porch, up the steps and into Katie's living room.

As soon as the screen door slammed behind her, Katie dropped her share of the burden unceremoniously onto the hardwood floor. John flinched as he let the man's shoulders and head down a little more easily. "I don't think torturing this guy is a good start toward making him listen to your side of the story."

Rider lifted a shaky hand to his head and rolled to his side.

"Are you awake?" Katie demanded, arms crossed over her chest as she glared down at the creature on the floor.

John shook his head in consternation as he knelt beside Rider and lifted one eyelid, then the other, then examined his head. When he touched the top left side, Rider flinched and grunted.

"He's coming around," John said. "His pupils look okay. I don't think you did any permanent damage."

"Too bad," Katie mumbled.

"You better be glad. I absolutely draw the line at helping you hide bodies."

Katie heaved a giant sigh. "I know, I know. I'm relieved I didn't kill the vermin. I just don't know what to do now. I've tried so hard to fix everything so the judge would see how stable I've become—this house, my job at the hospital, even a husband. Sort of a husband anyway. And now this jerk's going to ruin everything."

Rider opened his eyes and looked directly into hers. He was a good-looking specimen of vermin, she had to admit, with his chiseled features, too-long, shaggy brown hair and, she now saw, striking hazel eyes. It was too bad Mother Nature had squandered her artistic ability on someone like him.

He blinked, clutched his head and tried to sit up. John took his arm to help him.

"My head hurts," Rider complained.

"You had an accident." Katie sat on the floor beside him, her tone sarcastic. The accident was that she hadn't killed him.

"Who are you?" he asked.

She looked questioningly at John. He shrugged. "A little confusion isn't uncommon after a head injury."

Rider turned to look at John. "Who are you?"

"Do you know your name?" John asked.

Rider frowned. "No," he said after a moment of thought. "What's my name? Why can't I remember?"

"Just relax. Minor trauma to the head. In layman's terms, your brains are a little scrambled. It'll all come back soon."

"Do you know where you are?" Katie asked, drawing his attention to her again. Could she be so lucky that he had forgotten what he was here for? Dared she tempt fate and hope that his memory loss would last until after the hearing?

He looked around, then shook his head slowly. "No. Where am I?"

"Do you know what the date is?" John queried.

Rider drew a hand over his eyes and shook his head. "It's nineteen ninety something. I'm not sure."

"Do you know what city you're in?"

"No! Damn it, what's going on here? What's happened? Who are you? Who am I?"

"Who are you?" Katie considered the question, wondering if she had the guts to carry out the daring idea that had just popped into her head.

Yes, she decided. She could and would do whatever had to be done.

She cupped his chin gently in her hand, turned his face toward hers and smiled benignly. "Who are you? Why, you're my husband."

Chapter Two

John made a choking sound.

"Come on, *Fred,*" she said to him. "Let's help my husband, John, up off the floor, and then we can get him something for his headache." John's—the real John's—eyes widened. Actually, Katie reflected, *popped* would be a better description.

"I can get up by myself," Rider protested, pushing the two of them away.

John jerked his head toward the kitchen, his expression frantic.

"Okay, *dear,*" Katie said to Rider. "You get up by yourself, and we'll go find some water and an aspirin for you." She left the room with John close behind.

"Why on earth did you tell him he's your husband?" John demanded in hushed tones as soon as she had closed the door to the living room.

"Shhh!" She led him to the far corner of the big, old-fashioned kitchen. "This is my chance," she whispered. "I can talk to the enemy, explain the story, let him see that I'm really a good person, let him know what an injustice he'll be doing to Nathan if he sides with my parents. If I get him in the car and on the road, I'll have a captive audience even after he regains his memory."

"You're going to take him to Oklahoma with you? You can't do that! What if somebody's looking for him? What if he has a wife?"

"He doesn't have on a ring, so he probably doesn't. But what difference would that make? I don't want to marry him. I just want to borrow him for a little while. I imagine he'd planned to go up there for the hearing anyway, so it's not like he'll be going out of his way because of me. And by the time we get there, he'll be ready to help me, not my parents."

"You'll never get away with this. Memory loss like this is usually very temporary."

"How temporary?"

"Could be fifteen minutes, could be twenty-four hours."

"Twenty-four hours?"

"*Maybe.* It could be longer, but the point is, he could regain his memory any minute now. Maybe by the time we walk back out there. Maybe halfway across the Red River. A captive audience, yes, but a hostile one. Katie, you can't do this!"

Katie hesitated. Everything John said was true. But the alternative was even riskier. "I don't see that I have much choice. What do you want me to do? Go out there and tell him who he is and why he was peeking in my window and how I whacked him with a skillet, then give him back his tape recorder and let him ruin Nathan's life?"

John ran a hand through his hair and shook his head. "I guess not."

"Good. I knew I could count on you. Now first, do we need to take this creep to the emergency room? Not that I have much sympathy for him, but I'd hate to end up a murderer after all. Not to mention how inconvenient it'd be if he croaked in my car halfway to Oklahoma."

"I don't think he's going to die any time soon. If you take him to emergency, they'll check his pupils, which I already did, and tell him to take aspirin if his head continues to hurt. You do need to keep an eye on him, and if he passes out or you can't wake him up, get him to a hospital ASAP. But I don't think that's going to happen."

"Great. Now while I take him a glass of water and some aspirin, you go outside and get the tape recorder, that blasted contract and my skillet and take them with you." Thinking about the contract with its revelations reminded her of Rider's wallet. She pulled it from her pocket. "Put this in my glove compartment. No, wait."

She flipped it open and thumbed through.

"Katie, you shouldn't be going through his personal things," John protested.

"I almost killed the man. Going through his wallet can't be more personal than that. No pictures of a wife or kids. In case of emergency notify...Gary Rider. His father. And he lives in Austin. That's good. Here's my new husband's business card with his phone number." She picked up the telephone and dialed. After two rings, his answering machine picked up.

"This is Travis Rider. I'm not home. Leave a message."

"He's not married," Katie reported, hanging up the phone. "He said, 'I'm not home.' If he was married, his wife would have made him say *we*. So that takes care of that worry." She handed him the wallet. "Put this in my glove compartment, then load your luggage into the back seat of my car."

"My luggage? Why do you want my luggage?"

"You're pretty close to his size. Your clothes should fit. Can I borrow your identification, too, just in case?"

"No, you can't borrow my identification! And you can't have my clothes, either."

"I only want to borrow them. You packed for a couple of days, right? So you have plenty more at home. If I'm going to convince Travis Rider he's my husband, how am I going to explain to him why he doesn't have any clothes here? And what'll he do for clothes once we get up there? He can't go to court in that outfit he's wearing. At least, not if he switches to my side. If he won't listen to reason, he can go naked for all I care."

John expelled a long sigh. "All right. You can have the clothes, but not the identification."

It was more than she'd hoped for. "Deal. I'll figure out something on the ID if it comes up."

"Don't forget the ring."

"Oh, yeah. Thanks." Katie reached into her purse, took out the imitation-gold wedding band and slipped it onto her finger.

John shook his head. "I can't believe I'm helping you."

"I'll do the same for you."

"I know. You've always been there when I needed you. I just hope you never have occasion to repay this kind of a favor!"

"Relax. Everything's going to be fine. You go on out the back door and take care of things, and I'll get this cad a glass of water and two aspirin. And if he's remembered who he is, I'll pour the water over his head. With plenty of ice. It can't hurt matters at this point."

John. Somehow the name didn't seem to fit, but that was what the woman—his wife—had called him. He settled on the sofa, leaning back to ease the throbbing in his head.

Why the hell couldn't he remember who he was? The sensation of being lost in his own body was strange and awful. He couldn't remember who he was, couldn't remember his wife, couldn't remember his home... and he didn't particularly like his home now that he looked around.

The house itself was small and old while the furniture, pictures and area rugs appeared new though inexpensive. He must not make very much money as a...well, as whatever he did. And his wife wasn't much of a housekeeper. The place definitely had a lived-in look with its books, magazines, a pair of running shoes, a suitcase and garment bag—were they taking a trip?—a pencil and notepad...

"Here, John. Aspirin." His wife approached, tentatively holding a glass of ice water in one hand and two white pills in the other, both at arm's length.

Maybe she wasn't such a good housekeeper, but he could certainly see why he'd married her. She was a looker. Short, honey-colored hair, big eyes the shade of bluebonnets, full pink lips, fair skin with a golden glow as if she spent a lot of time in the sun, thin cotton shirt outlining round breasts that would just fit in a man's hand, and faded blue jeans wrapped snugly around a rear to match those breasts. Damn! How could a man forget a woman like that?

He couldn't keep the smile from his lips as he accepted the water and the pills. "Thanks, uh, honey." Her enormous eyes got even bigger. Had he said something wrong? Maybe he didn't normally call her *honey.* But he didn't know her name.

He tossed the aspirins into his mouth, washing them down with the cold water. The sensation of a cool liquid trickling down his throat was real and tangible and familiar in this strange, unreal, out-of-focus world.

She sat beside him. "How do you feel?"

"Weird," he said. "But much better with you here." He did sense some sort of connection between the two of them, but it was only a feeling. He couldn't pull the facts out of the mist of his memory. He moved closer, wanting to strengthen that connection. "You smell good. Kind of like...uh..."

"Honeysuckle," she supplied, inching away from him as if frightened. "You still don't know who you are, do you?"

"No, I'm sorry." He couldn't blame her for being a little freaked out with the whole thing; he certainly was. "I know there's something between us, but I still don't remember you. I don't even know your name."

"It's Katie Logan. Katie Logan Dunn. That's your name. Dunn. John Dunn. We're married. Two days ago." She held out her left hand to show him the plain gold band. A pretty cheap-looking gold band. Was that the best he could afford?

"Katie." He tried the name, rolling it off his tongue. "John Dunn. Katie Dunn." Neither name rang any bells. In fact, they both sounded kind of flat to his ears. Oh, well. Most people disliked their names.

He brightened at that thought. At least he remembered generalizations. Things could be worse.

He smiled, his gaze sweeping from her shiny blond hair down the length of her slim body. "I certainly do have good taste, wife."

She fidgeted nervously for a moment, staring at her hands in her lap, then took a deep breath. "Look, maybe we better take you to emergency and get an X ray or brain scan or something."

"For a little bump on the head like this? No way." He couldn't remember any details, but he sensed that his experiences with hospitals hadn't been pleasant. He definitely had no desire to go to one for something as minor as this injury. "Don't worry. Like that other guy said, I'm just a little confused after the accident. I'll be all right in a few minutes."

He reached to take her slim hand in his. Her fingers were as icy as the water he'd just drunk. Could be from carrying the glass. Or could be from concern about him. He kind of liked that.

The screen door opened. Katie jerked her hand away as the other guy—Fred, she'd called him—charged in, his face flushed. "Okay, Katie, you're all set."

John frowned. Was his injured mind playing more tricks? "Didn't you go through there a few minutes ago?" He jerked his thumb toward the rear of the house.

"Back door," Katie supplied. "He went out the back door and came in the front."

"Why?"

"He was . . . putting up the ladder. The one you fell off of."

"I fell off a ladder? At night? What was I doing on a ladder in the dark?"

"You were . . ." She hesitated, giving Fred a desperate look. What the hell could he have been doing on a ladder that she didn't want to tell him about? "Rescuing the cat," she finished. "He got stuck on the roof."

"We have a cat?" The very thought made him want to sneeze.

"I have a cat. I had it before we got married."

"So where is he now?"

"He ran off when you fell. But he'll be back. You know what they say about the cat always coming back."

He lifted a hand to the lump that was forming on his head and frowned. She sounded a little *off,* her words too bright, out of sync . . . he wasn't sure. Something was wrong, though he couldn't say exactly what.

Well, hell, losing his memory was wrong. What more did he want? Katie was doing the best she could. He had no reason to be suspicious of her.

Katie cast Fred a worried look. "Maybe we ought to get him to a doctor after all."

"I may not remember my name right now, but I'm pretty sure I'm an adult male of legal age and capable of making my own decisions, and I said I don't need to go to a doctor." The very idea set his teeth on edge. "I'll let you know if I change my mind. And don't talk about me as if I weren't here."

Fred shrugged. "There's not much they could do anyway. If the pain gets worse, you probably ought to see a doctor, but you seem to be doing okay."

"Fred's a doctor," Katie explained. "So are you. You and Fred work together. You're residents at Springcreek General Hospital."

"I'm a doctor?" That surprised him. More strongly than ever, he felt an instinctive aversion to hospitals. But maybe that was why—working with sick people all the time. "Do I like being a doctor?"

"You love it," Katie declared. "Except the long hours you put in as a resident."

He supposed that would explain the aversion. Still...

Fred shifted uncomfortably from one foot to the other. "I need to go, Katie. I've got to get back on duty at the hospital."

"Don't worry about me," John assured him. "I'm feeling better already."

Katie bounced to her feet. "Great. Then we can get started. We've got a three-hour drive tonight, and it's already nearly ten. Bye, Fred."

"Bye, Katie. Bye, uh, John." Fred left in a hurry.

"I hope he doesn't get to work late because he stayed to take care of me."

"He'll be okay. Well, are you about ready to hit the road?" She stooped and picked up the suitcase and garment bag.

John rose, too, and took them from her. "Where are we going?"

"Hillsdale, Oklahoma. We're in Dallas now. It's a long story. I'll tell you on the way up there."

He followed her out to the small blue car parked on the street in front of the house—a new car. If he was only a resident, probably with a heavy debt load, and they'd just gotten married, he could understand why they couldn't afford the best. But why was everything so new? Hadn't either of them had a life until recently?

Again he had that nagging sensation that things were just a little awry, like a jigsaw puzzle with the pieces forced in where they didn't fit.

"You can throw my bags in the back seat with yours," Katie instructed. He started toward the driver's side, but she laid a gentle hand on his arm. "Under the circumstances, I think I'd better drive."

He didn't much like the idea of someone else driving, but he had to admit she was right. He nodded and tossed her bags into the back, then climbed in beside her.

Katie held her breath as she watched Rider squeezing his big frame into the passenger seat of her car. Was she really going to be lucky enough to get away with this? If it worked, she'd know for sure Becky had sent down a guardian angel to protect her son. Any other explanation was too far out to believe.

"This car wasn't made for people my size," he observed, one leg still outside the door.

"I know. I bought it before we got married."

"Where's my car? Is it bigger?"

"Yes." That was a safe answer. Most cars were. As to where it was, that was a good question. Parked up the block, hidden from view of her house? "It's...it's in the shop."

"Oh." He flinched as he tugged his second leg into the car, drawing the knee up fairly close to his chin.

"You're really uncomfortable, aren't you? Maybe you should ride in the back. Sit sideways." Much as he deserved to be uncomfortable, she wanted him to be receptive to what she had to tell him.

"I'm okay. It's just that I seem to have some bruises on my, uh, backside, too. I must have taken a heck of a fall."

With only the barest trace of guilt, Katie remembered the way she'd lugged him across the ground before dropping him onto the floor. "I'll drive fast, get there as quickly as possible." Even in the faint glow from the streetlight, she could see the disapproval on his face. "Just kidding." She hadn't been, but she supposed stable people drove the speed limit. "Just relax and lean back. Everything's under control." For the moment.

She started the car and headed down the deserted street toward Highway 75. This was her chance. Even if he regained his memory in the next five minutes, he was now trapped with her inside a moving car.

"We're going to a custody hearing," she began. "For my orphaned nephew, Nathan Anderson. It's critical that I win and not my parents."

"Whew. We just got married and already we're going to have a son." He laughed nervously. "I suppose we talked about this before we got married."

She cast a glance at him out of the corner of her eye. Obviously, the role of father wasn't comfortable for him. Thank goodness he wasn't going to be Nathan's father for real! "Oh, yes. You knew all about Nathan."

"How old is our potential child?"

"He's eight, and he's a sweetie. Let me tell you the story from the beginning, so you'll understand why this is so important."

"Fire away. Maybe when I hear familiar stuff, my memory will start coming back."

That might be, but she'd be willing to bet Travis Rider wasn't familiar with anything she was about to tell him.

Katie wheeled around a corner, and Rider grunted. "Sorry," she said. "I'll try to be more careful." Though he couldn't have been slung around too much the way he was wedged in. "Okay," she began. "Twenty-eight years ago, I was born to Ralph and Nadine Logan in Hillsdale, Oklahoma. My impending birth was the reason they got married. I'm not quite sure how I happened. I know they don't believe in birth control, but I'd have sworn they didn't believe in sex, either. Anyway, they must have lost control a couple of times because I had a sister three years later. Katherine and Rebecca, they named us, though we go by Katie and Becky. At least, she went by Becky until she died three months ago."

Katie bit her lip. It was still hard to talk about Becky without crying. Too bad she hadn't inherited her parents' stoic control.

No, she corrected herself, it wasn't too bad. She'd rather cry her eyes out than be like them.

"How'd Becky die?" Rider asked softly.

"Defective space heater. She and her husband, Darryl, died in their sleep. Nathan was spending the night with one of his friends. But I'm getting ahead of my story."

She checked the traffic, then accelerated up the entrance ramp onto Highway 75.

"Central Expressway's always busy," she grumbled. "If you've forgotten the traffic jams on this highway, you're really in bad shape!"

He laughed. It was a nice laugh. Without his memory, Travis Rider seemed to be a decent fellow. "I guess I'm in bad shape, then. I don't remember. So tell me the rest of your story."

She took a deep breath. "I'm sure my parents loved us in their own way." Actually, she wasn't at all sure of that fact, but it *might* be true. "However, neither of them ever forgave the other or me for what happened. The humiliation of having to get married and then the arrival of a seven-month-old baby."

"Your parents must be pretty old-fashioned. Even as little as I remember, that doesn't matter to most people anymore."

"My parents are old-fashioned, stern, rigid people, especially my father. And Mother goes along with anything he says. They were both determined that neither of their children would make the same mistake they made. We worked hard, studied hard, came straight home from school, had no friends, ate everything on our plates, didn't talk at meals, or between meals for that matter, didn't make any decisions, not even what to wear to school or how to wear our hair. We had no affection, only rules."

She paused, wondering if she was saying the right words to make him understand the cold, lonely world she'd grown up in.

Rider laid a comforting hand on her shoulder, and she flashed him a quick smile.

"How did you ever get the courage to escape?" he asked.

"I wasn't very old when I figured out that the way we lived wasn't normal. I saw how other kids lived, and I wanted to be like that. At night, Becky and I would huddle under the covers and talk. I became pretty rebellious. As soon as I graduated from high school, I ran away from home. I promised Becky I'd make enough money to send for her."

"And did you?"

"Yeah, kind of. I made my way to Dallas and worked as a waitress, two jobs at a time, and by the end of a year I had a tiny apartment, a car with four bald tires and no heater and a little money in the bank. But by then Becky was pregnant. How she ever managed to accomplish that while living in the same house with Mother and Father is beyond me! But she did, and she and Darryl ran away and got married and moved in with Darryl's parents until he graduated from high school."

"Nathan," Rider guessed.

Katie smiled, her eyes on the yellow line of the highway, but her thoughts going back to the first time she'd seen the wrinkled red baby. "Yep. Nathan came into the world. They let Darryl and me both be there for his birth. Becky said she wouldn't go through with it if they didn't." She blinked back the sudden mist that threatened her vision. "You never saw three prouder parents! All the time she was pregnant, Becky swore she'd see to it that her baby always felt loved. After he got there, it wasn't even a matter of choice. Nobody can help but love a baby. Well, nobody but my parents."

"Who love in their own way," Rider reminded her.

"Yeah, well, sort of, I guess. Anyway, Becky was happy, and I decided I would be, too. I made up my mind to do everything I'd always thought about doing, to live life with no restraints and no one telling me I couldn't do something. I got a job as a flight attendant and flew around the world for a couple of years.

That was fun. Then I spent a year in the Amazon rain forest with a study group. After that, I backpacked across Europe, went on a fossil dig in Africa, helped with a housing project for the poor in Mexico, learned to ski in Colorado and to surf in California, and anything else I took a notion to do. It was great. Whenever I got bored or started feeling hemmed in, I'd just go on to something else. And in between, I worked at odd jobs in Dallas and always managed to make time to spend with Nathan."

"Sounds like you and Nathan are pretty tight."

"Yeah. He kinda likes his Aunt Katie."

"So what's the custody deal about? Wouldn't your sister have wanted you to have custody?"

"She and Darryl always said if anything happened to them, I should take Nathan." Her hands gripped the steering wheel convulsively, hanging on. "But they were so young, they thought they were invulnerable. They never got around to putting it in writing. Darryl's parents know, and they're going to testify for me."

"That should work, shouldn't it?"

"Not necessarily. My parents are determined to get custody so they can correct the frivolous, permissive way Becky was raising their grandchild. They're pillars of the community. My father's a vice president at the bank and a deacon in the church. I wasn't there when Becky and Darryl died, and my parents snatched Nathan up and filed a motion for temporary then permanent custody. Darryl's parents heard about it in time and intervened to at least get visitation for me and for themselves."

"Are they trying to get custody, too?"

"No, they're testifying for me and they don't want to muddy the waters. Anyway, they're in their sixties, retired, and they'd never say they're too old, but they did say they thought Nathan needed a younger parent. So my father managed to snare temporary custody, and then he refused to let me see Nathan."

"How could he refuse if the court gave you the right?"

He really did have amnesia, she thought wryly. "Men like my father have no problem defying court orders. He didn't bring Nathan to Becky and Darryl's funeral, and every time I drove up there, he wouldn't open the door. The permanent custody hearing was scheduled for sooner than I could have gotten a contempt motion on the docket. Tomorrow the judge decides the permanent custody. And my parents are saying my life-style shows I'm flaky, irresponsible and not stable enough to raise a child."

"Well, I don't know if I'd go that far," Rider said carefully, "but I have to admit, it doesn't sound as if you could ever be a member of the PTA and coach the soccer team."

Katie clenched her teeth. He might have amnesia, but he was still a jerk.

"I can do whatever it takes to make sure Nathan is happy. Since Becky and Darryl died at the same time and I was secondary beneficiary on both policies, I had enough money to buy a house."

"So if they made you secondary beneficiary, doesn't that prove they intended for you to take care of their son?"

"My lawyer says it shows intent, but it's still not legal proof." Her fingers tightened around the steering wheel, squeezing the hard surface in frustration.

"They thought they were being so careful. They were worried that if they made Nathan the beneficiary, if anything happened while he was a minor, our parents might somehow get control of the money as court-appointed trustees or something."

"If they were worried enough to take out insurance policies and think it through to that extent, why didn't they make a will?"

"They didn't take out the insurance policies. They both worked at the same plant, and the insurance came with the job. They thought it all out because it was right in front of them, a choice they had to make. Writing a will, finding a lawyer, getting an appointment—that's different. That's something you have to think about and plan, and they weren't planning to die." Flooring the accelerator, she swung around a car that was going entirely too slow.

Rider touched her forearm. "Easy, honey," he said. "I don't plan to die any time soon, either."

"Sorry." She raised her foot a good quarter inch, forcibly reminding herself that speed for fun was one thing, but speed to release anger wasn't very smart. "Anyway, to continue with my respectability saga, I'd been friends with Jo—with Fred for years, and he helped me arrange to take a crash course in being a medical transcriptionist, then he helped me get a job at Springcreek General Hospital."

"Where I'm a resident. Is that where we met?"

Katie swallowed hard and kept her eyes riveted on the road ahead. She'd become so engrossed in making Travis Rider understand and believe the truth, that telling a lie—even in a just cause and even after she'd told so many tonight—suddenly didn't feel right.

"If not for this custody thing, I'd never have met you." That was true enough.

"Katie..." He sounded oddly tentative. "Did we get married just for this hearing? Is this a marriage of convenience?"

"I'd never marry anyone for that kind of a reason." In fact, she'd never actually marry anyone—give up control of her own life—for any kind of a reason. When the caseworker had admitted that being single would be a strike against her, she'd impulsively told the woman she was engaged, knowing she'd have to lie because it would never happen for real.

"I sure am glad to hear that." Rider lifted his hand to her cheek, stroking gently with his knuckles, then letting his fingers trail lazily down her neck, over her shoulder and along her arm. To her surprise and chagrin, she didn't flinch from his touch. Instead, she found herself enjoying it, wanting more, her breath coming a little faster as currents of electricity zigzagged through her body. The sensation was insane and wonderful. She could only compare it to the first time she'd caught the crest of a wave and surfed in to shore.

How was that possible? How could she enjoy the touch of a man who worked for her parents, a man who'd set out to ruin everything?

Travis Rider might give her the same sensations as surfing, but she suspected these feelings were a lot more dangerous.

"Where are we spending the night?" he asked.

"In the Sleepy Time Motel." She was barely able to squeeze the words up through her throat. She'd made reservations for John—the real John—and herself. She had a sleeping bag in the trunk of the car, which

John had gallantly offered to use. No problem. He was like a brother. They'd gone camping and shared the same tent before.

But this wasn't the real John Dunn. This was a man who believed he was her husband. This was a man she feared and disliked. This was a man to whom, it seemed, she was as strongly drawn as she was to speeding around a sharp curve so fast she could feel two wheels lift off the ground.

Okay, Becky, she thought frantically, *call off the angel. I got our message across. Give him back his memory. Fast. Sometime before we reach Hillsdale. And that motel.*

Chapter Three

Even before he'd asked the question about their marriage, John had felt on an instinctive level that Katie hadn't married him just to get custody of her nephew. She was a good person, an honorable person; he knew that from listening to her, being with her, even though right now he had nothing concrete in his memory on which to base that judgment.

Not to mention that she was a damned attractive woman. He was definitely looking forward to getting to that motel. His head still ached a little and his brain still refused to cough up his memories, but the rest of his body was in perfect working order.

"Want me to drive for a while?" he offered. "You can tell me where to turn."

"We're almost there. Thanks anyway. You ought to try to get some rest after your accident. Tomorrow's a big day, and with this late start, tonight's going to be a short night. Just lie back. Take a nap."

She seemed a little nervous. Of course, having your husband of only two days fall off a ladder and forget all about you was probably enough to make anybody nervous.

"I'm not tired," he assured her. "Tell me more about us, about me. This is really weird, being a stranger to myself. How old am I? Where'd I go to school? Was I born in Dallas?"

"Is anybody born in Dallas? You know, I hate to tell you everything because then when your memory starts coming back, how will you know what you've remembered and what I've told you? Why don't we listen to some music?" She turned on the radio and tuned in an oldies station.

"Katie," he said impatiently, "I need to know at least a little bit about myself to be able to function. What if I still don't remember everything by tomorrow? How am I going to be able to deal with your family if I don't know who I am?"

"You won't be able to deal with my family no matter what. Anyway, all the medical journals recommend that you tell an amnesia patient as little as possible. You should know that. You're a doctor."

"Well, I don't know that. I don't know anything, and I don't like the feeling." He sighed in resignation. "All right. But I'd just as soon we kept this problem to ourselves. I don't want the whole world to know I can't even remember my name."

"Good idea." She sounded relieved.

He leaned back to the extent the miniature car would allow and let the music flow over him as he studied her profile and drank in the closeness of her presence. Outside, the dark world flew past them—she might be going a little over the speed limit—as they drove into the night, the only two people in the world so far as he could tell.

He was a doctor with a beautiful, exciting wife. He felt a little shaky about the kid they were going to acquire, but he must have known about Nathan before he married Katie. He must have thought it was a workable deal. It would be again as soon as he remembered everything.

Yeah, it appeared he had a life worth remembering, his aversion to hospitals notwithstanding. Surely when he got his memory back, he'd be okay with that part, too—even if the idea still sent shudders through him right now.

As they drove on through the darkness, the little car seemed to become smaller, squeezing John's frame more and more tightly. If they had to take any more trips, it would have to be in his car.

Finally, Katie exited the highway. "Here we are," she said, sounding bright and perky, though he knew she must be exhausted. "The big city of Hillsdale, population ten thousand or thereabouts. How are you feeling? Any change?" Her voice became tentative.

"I feel all right. Headache's practically gone." Or maybe it was just obscured by the pains in the rest of his cramped body. "Is that our motel up ahead?"

"That's it. The Sleepy Time Motel." Her voice squeaked slightly. She pulled into the parking lot and stopped. "Well, here we are." She drew one finger slowly around the steering wheel, her attention focused on the movement. "I already said that, didn't I?"

He caught her hand in his. "Relax, babe. Everything's going to work out just fine tomorrow."

She looked at him then, her eyes desperately searching his face. He tucked one finger under her chin and smiled at her. "I may not have any control over the judge, but I can promise I'll be the ideal picture of a husband. By morning, I'll be myself again anyway." Oddly, that didn't seem to comfort her. "But if I'm not, I'll fake it," he reassured her. "We'll be perfect parents. You don't have a thing to worry about. Okay?"

She nodded, though the worried expression on her face didn't change.

John opened his door, expecting his restricted body to burst into the sudden freedom, but his limbs had stiffened in place. As he carefully stretched out his legs, the release felt excruciatingly wonderful. "I'll go check us in," he said, reveling in the open expanse of balmy night air around him as he crawled from the enclosure.

"No!"

Her urgent tone pulled his attention back to her. She gazed at him from wide, uncertain eyes, and she hadn't moved from her position behind the steering wheel.

"I'll go," she said. "You stay here and rest."

"Katie, I don't need to rest, and if I did, this car would be the last place in the world I could do it. If you're worried about me, come on. We'll both go in."

As she preceded him to the office, he placed a hand at her waist, an affectionate, proprietary gesture. Nice. Walking through the warm summer night behind his wife with his hand on her waist. But she could have been a stranger until three hours ago for all the familiarity the act stirred.

Katie pushed the buzzer to summon the night clerk, and John reached into his back pocket for his wallet.

His pocket was empty.

He tried the other one, then both front pockets.

"What's the matter?" Katie asked.

"I can't find my wallet." He checked his jacket.

"What do you need with your wallet?"

"To pay for the room, just for starters," he said irritably. "Surely I have a wallet with credit cards and driver's license. It's a good thing I *didn't* drive on the way up here. Do you have any idea what could have happened to it?"

"Yes. Yes, I do."

He looked at her expectantly, but she didn't continue. She had that cornered-rabbit look again, just like before she got out of the car. What the devil was going on? "And do you want to share that information with me?" he encouraged.

"Your wallet . . . is gone."

"I noticed." What could have happened to make her so reluctant to tell him? Had she hidden his wallet for some reason? Maybe to keep him from driving up here with his injury?

"Someone took it out of your pocket."

"A pickpocket lifted my wallet?" For some reason, he found that hard to believe. But he supposed everyone assumed they were too clever, too alert, to fall victim to a crime like that.

"I can see you've forgotten the incident."

"I've forgotten everything," he said wryly. "Remember?"

A small white-haired man wearing a plaid robe and still rubbing sleep from his eyes entered from the back room and unlocked the door to admit them into the office. "You folks need a room?"

"Yes. I have reservations for Mr. and Mrs. John Dunn."

"Oh, yeah. I'd about give you folks up."

"We had a long trip getting here." Katie handed the man a credit card.

"This here says 'Katherine Logan,'" the man protested, eyeing the card as well as the two of them suspiciously.

Katie moved closer to John and took his arm. He covered her hand with his and smiled down at her. "We just got married," she explained, flashing the ring on her left hand, then releasing him to reach inside her purse. "Here's a copy of the marriage license." She handed him a folded piece of paper.

She carried a copy of their license with her? That was odd.

To John's surprise, instead of returning it at once, the man unfolded the paper, fitted glasses onto his nose and examined it. John couldn't remember much about his own life, but he was pretty sure society no longer cared if a man and woman spending the night together in a motel were married or not. Except this was a small town. Maybe things were different here.

"Newlyweds, huh?" He handed Katie the paper and John a key. "One thirty-three. Around back. Don't be burning no holes in my sheets." He grinned and winked.

Katie cringed and blushed.

Resenting the old man's sleazy attitude, John wrapped a protective arm around Katie's slim, rigid shoulders. How dare the man embarrass someone as obviously innocent as his Katie?

"Come on, honey," he said gently. Maybe he couldn't recall what he ate for breakfast this morning, but he could still take care of his wife.

Katie walked woodenly through the door of room 133 of the Sleepy Time Motel. The place could have been carpeted in rainbow colors with neon signs on the walls for all she knew. Her field of vision encompassed nothing except that double bed. That tiny rectangle.

Her logic in requesting the one double had been that a newly married couple sleeping in two beds might have aroused suspicion, but why hadn't she asked for king-size?

Rider walked around her and dropped their luggage to the floor. She could see that he'd take up at least two-thirds of the bed. There'd be nowhere to get away from him.

He turned and smiled at her, then walked around to close the door behind her. She stood motionless, paralyzed. Not that there would be anywhere to go if she decided to move.

She jumped at the feel of warm fingers on her shoulders. "You're really tense," Rider said. "Come sit down and let me rub your neck."

He strode across the room and pulled down the covers.

"Come on." He patted the white sheet. "You did all the driving. Now it's your turn to relax. After all, you've got a big day ahead of you tomorrow."

The air-conditioning unit whirred beside her, but the refrigerated breeze didn't make a dent in the heat that started somewhere inside and worked its way to her skin. "Uh, John..." Maybe she ought to tell him the truth. She'd had her opportunity to plead her side of the case. Her original idea had been a good one. She still believed that. She just hadn't planned beyond the pleading part of things. And now they were beyond it. Way beyond.

He took her hand and drew her to the bed, then gently pushed her down. She popped up again.

"We need to..." She didn't have a clue what they needed to do. If she'd known before, the act of standing so close to Travis Rider in the tiny motel room, next to the tiny bed, had driven the thought right out of her mind.

"We need to what?"

She sank back onto the bed. At least that way she wasn't so close to him.

He knelt in front of her and began to untie the laces of one canvas shoe.

"Talk!" she exclaimed. "We need to talk."

"Okay. Talk." He removed her shoes and lifted her legs onto the bed.

She watched like a rabbit mesmerized by a snake as he tossed his leather jacket onto a chair, then took off his own shoes and socks and slid in behind her, leaning against the headboard and wrapping his long legs around her.

Talk. They needed to talk.

Expertly he began to massage her neck, his strong fingers picking out spots she hadn't even realized were tense. The corners of the room softened and rounded as did the sharp edges and corners of her mind. She was tired, so tired, and not just from the drive. The past three months had been frenzied, hectic, nerve-racking.

Travis Rider's skillful fingers reached that frenzy, soothed those frayed nerves. His touch was gentle and sure as he cradled her between his black denim-covered legs.

Maybe she could allow herself to relax for just a minute or two. What could it hurt? She'd probably be able to think more clearly, to get everything straightened out if she were calmer.

She allowed herself to sink into the delicious sensations. The solid bed beneath her melted away, and she seemed to be floating on a cloud, anchored only to Travis's fingers, Travis's legs around her, Travis's chest against her back, Travis's breath warm on her neck.

Maybe, she thought hazily, she ought to let him get a good night's sleep—what was left of the night anyway—before hitting him with the truth.

There. She was thinking more clearly already.

He tipped her forward gently, holding her shoulder with one hand while the fingers of the other traveled slowly down her back, caressing and massaging each segment of her spine. The sensation was exquisite. She'd never before felt so relaxed yet so acutely aware at the same time.

His hand reached the small of her back, the waistband of her blue jeans, slid under her T-shirt and began the trip upward, the sensations intensified a thousandfold by the contact of his flesh against hers.

It was a little like riding in a hot-air balloon—floating free of the earth, no bonds, no restrictions, yet preternaturally aware of the wind against your body, the brilliant blue sky above, the vibrant green fields below, all sounds stilled, the air hushed.

His hands molded to her shoulders, squeezing, pressing, stroking, his fingers sliding around her ribs, under her bra, caressing the sides of her breasts. Something on the periphery of her mind warned her that that wasn't good, but her body liked it just fine.

He tipped her sideways and leaned over to touch her lips with his, taking her ever higher. Surfing, skiing, hot-air ballooning, shooting the rapids—nothing compared to this. She wrapped an arm around his neck and pulled herself closer, wanting more, wanting all he had to offer.

At her movement, his kiss became ravenous, and she responded eagerly, parting her lips, inviting him inside. He accepted the invitation, his tongue sliding in to explore the depths of her mouth, setting all her nerves whirling in ecstasy.

His hand tangled in her hair as his lips moved downward to her throat, trailing passionate kisses, setting off chain reactions of tingles that spread throughout her body, making every inch of her ultrasensitive in their wake. She felt his fingers behind her again, tugging at her bra, then the welcome release of the garment.

He twisted around, laying her across the bed, leaning over her, his eyes narrow slits of desire. "Oh, sweetheart," he whispered, "that must have been some kind of a bump to make me forget a woman like you."

"Omigosh!" Katie shot up to a sitting position as though spring-loaded, her action pushing him aside, almost toppling him from the bed.

What on earth was she doing? It simply wasn't possible she'd been about to make love with the detective hired by her parents, the man who'd been spying on her only a few hours ago. She scrambled off the bed and made a mad dash into the bathroom, slamming the door behind her.

"Katie! What's the matter?"

"Nothing!" She turned on the cold water full force and splashed it onto her face, but it wasn't enough to cool down her embarrassment, her fear...or that inexplicable desire.

"Can I come in?"

"No!" She sank onto the tile floor. There was only a shower, not even a tub to sit on...or to sleep in. Thanks to her clever scheming and quick thinking, the only place she could sleep tonight was in that little bitty double bed, next to Travis's hot body.

One o'clock in the morning, and the hearing was at nine. That meant at least six hours in that bed. It was going to be a long night after all.

Wearing only his black briefs, uncovered and with the air conditioner turned on full blast, John was still uncomfortably warm as he lay beside Katie and watched the motel room gradually begin to lighten with the dawn. He'd been awake all night, puzzled by her strange behavior and achingly aware of her fully clothed body only inches away.

What the hell was going on with his wife? She'd changed her blue jeans for a pair of tights and kept on her T-shirt. Not exactly the sort of thing a new bride usually wore. He didn't for a minute buy her story that she was worried making love would complicate his head injury.

Was it possible, in this day and age, that Katie and he hadn't consummated their relationship, not even on their wedding night? Was she frightened of making love? That didn't fit, either. She hadn't been frightened when he'd kissed her. At that moment, he'd been certain they enjoyed a torrid sex life.

There was something she wasn't telling him. He was sure of it. What was it that made those big blue eyes widen with what—panic?—when they got out of the car, when he mentioned his wallet.

If he could only remember! But it seemed the harder he tried, the more elusive the memories became.

He eased out of bed, being careful not to wake her. With a final look at her slim body hugging her side of the mattress convulsively, he took his shaving kit from his suitcase and went in to take a shower—a cold one.

As he soaped his chest, his fingers hit a ridge of irregular tissue. Looking down, he noticed two jagged scars, one on the left side of his chest and a longer one running diagonally across his stomach.

Knife wounds, he thought, and wasn't sure if the knowledge came from a partial memory of the event or of his medical knowledge as a doctor. Either way, he didn't think such wounds came from his medical training.

As he shampooed his hair, his fingers touched the lump on the side of his head. It was still tender to the touch, but the headache had gone away. Surely that was a good sign. Surely he'd start remembering things any time now.

He dried off, stepped outside the shower and stared at himself in the mirror. Scars from knife wounds, bloodshot eyes, a heavy growth of dark beard and a scowl. He didn't look much like someone to whom a judge would award custody of an eight-year-old child. A shave, a little Visine and a cup of coffee should improve matters.

He opened his shaving kit. No Visine.

There it was—a memory! He was sure he carried Visine at all times. After a long night's work, his eyes were always red.

He concentrated, reaching for more, but that was all. Big deal. What good was it to remember that he got bloodshot eyes after working all night? Everybody knew that residents worked crazy hours, and he could see the evidence of what happened after a sleepless night right in front of him.

And his Visine had gone the way of his wallet. Maybe a pickpocket got it, too, he thought wryly. They probably kept late hours in that line of work.

He took out a razor and shaved. Digging around in his shaving kit, he located a half-empty bottle of after-shave and splashed on a little. When the fumes assaulted his nose, he looked closely at the unfamiliar bottle.

That bump on the head must have done something to his olfactory nerves. Undoubtedly he'd liked this scent before, but right now it smelled like gun cleaner.

Maybe Katie had given it to him, and he didn't want to hurt her feelings by not using it.

He sniffed the bottle again.

And just how, he wondered, did he know what gun cleaner smelled like? Wouldn't he have been more likely to identify it with a medicine smell?

A knife wound and gun cleaner. Instead of finding answers as time went along, he kept coming up with more questions.

As soon as this hearing was over, he probably should conquer his distaste of hospitals and go see a doctor to get one of those things where they tested the brain.

He shook his head in disgust. He was a doctor, and the best terminology he could come up with was *one of those things where they tested the brain.*

He opened the bathroom door and headed for his suitcase to get some clean underwear.

Katie was awake and sitting cross-legged in the middle of the bed eating a chocolate-covered doughnut. She turned a bright red, choked and looked away.

He was no longer so sure about his wonderful life. Katie definitely had some major hang-ups, they apparently had no sex life, and he was positive something else was going on that she wasn't telling him about.

"Sorry," he mumbled. He opened his suitcase and took out a pair of white boxer shorts. From black briefs to white boxer shorts? They weren't new, so he must have worn them before. He pulled them on. They felt funny, kind of loose and flowing in the breeze.

"I went out and got us some breakfast," Katie said, her back still turned to him. "This little shop has the best doughnuts in the world."

"Great." After the night he'd just spent, he could have used some real food—eggs, sausages, biscuits—but he'd hate for her to think he didn't appreciate her gesture. He opened his garment bag and grimaced as he took out the blue suit, white shirt and paisley tie. Oh, well. It would be appropriate attire for a custody hearing.

Katie could hear the rustle of clothing behind her as Travis dressed. She didn't dare look. That glimpse of him coming out of the bathroom naked, the dark mat of hair on his chest still wet and glistening, was more than enough to send her composure into hiding.

"How's your head?" she asked. That was a much safer area of his body to focus on.

"My head? My head's okay. Katie, did we use new dry cleaners the last time we had this suit cleaned?" he asked, his voice calm but strained.

"Why? Is it dirty?" She ventured a glance in his direction. He was dressed in John's best blue suit... and the sleeves and pants were a good inch too short.

"Everything seems to have shrunk," he said.

"Yes," she agreed, her mind racing frantically to try to find an explanation. "So it would appear."

He sank onto the side of the bed and grunted as he tried to fit one foot into John's dress shoe. "So have my shoes."

Maybe she could convince him he'd sustained total body swelling as a result of his accident.

Maybe she should tell him the truth.

She only had three hours until the hearing to decide what to do.

"Katie, are these things really my clothes?"

"No," she said, snatching the opportunity gratefully. Deceit really wasn't her thing. She'd feel much better when everything was out in the open. "No, those are not your clothes. They belong to the guy you met at my house."

"Fred?" He frowned, looking dark and ominous, and she was reminded of his role in the drama coming up. He could be merciless if he testified against her. Three more hours until the hearing. If she waited until afterward to tell him, she could be sure he wouldn't say anything damaging about her. It was highly unlikely her parents had ever met him. They never ventured out of their own little domain, and the contract she'd seen had been sent through the mail.

"What am I doing with Fred's clothes?" Travis asked, the distrust clear in his voice and on his face.

"I borrowed them for you." That was true.

"Don't I have a suit of my own?"

"Would you have had to borrow Fred's if you did?"

He stared at her so intently she had to look away before the strength of his gaze pulled the truth from her.

"I guess not," he finally said. "Well, I can't wear these shoes. I'll have to wear my sneakers. At least they're black. Maybe I can slip out at lunch and buy some new clothes." He yanked his shoelaces tight. "Damn! I don't have any money or credit cards."

"You can use mine." It was the least she could do. Maybe if she bought him a new outfit, he'd feel a little bit obligated and not be quite so angry when he found out the truth.

He scowled up at her, and for a moment she thought he could read her thoughts. "I can't take your credit cards," he said.

"Oh, stop that macho garbage. Married people have joint accounts."

"I guess you're right," he said, though he still sounded a little dubious. He straightened from tying his shoes and looked around. "Did you bring any coffee with those doughnuts?"

"Oh, dear. No, just a six-pack of cola. I, uh, forgot you drink coffee."

"It's okay. We can stop on the way into town."

Now she felt guilty again. He was being so accommodating, and she knew he probably needed his caffeine as much as she needed hers. She didn't think he'd gotten any more sleep than she had last night—which was none.

But she couldn't afford to feel guilty. He hadn't been so accommodating when he'd been snooping around her house, gathering evidence to condemn a little boy to an unhappy childhood. As soon as he got his memory back, he'd return to being a jerk.

Her original plan just to get to tell her side of the story was a good one, but this bonus of actually having him appear as her husband was fate—not to mention justice, considering what he'd been trying to do. Becky and her guardian angel were doing their best to look out for Nathan's welfare. She could scarcely defy an arrangement like that, however uncomfortable it made her.

He sank to the bed beside her and took a glazed doughnut. "Katie, where did I get those scars on my chest and stomach? Was I in a knife fight?"

Katie gasped, her teeth clenching as she bit into her second pastry. Jelly oozed all over her chin, fingers and lap.

"Katie?"

She swallowed the chunk of doughnut without even chewing. "I don't know. You never told me about it."

A knife fight? As if things weren't bad enough, now she has to learn the man she was sleeping with—and lying to—participated in knife fights.

A knock—no, a pounding—on the motel room door finished off Katie's already jangled nerves. She squeaked and dropped the rest of her doughnut on the bed.

Travis laid a comforting hand on her shoulder. "I'll see who it is."

She watched him walk across the room, managing to look in control in spite of the ill-fitting clothes and the situation. She didn't need to see who was at the door. The imperative, demanding nature of the pounding left no doubt in her mind.

"Who are you?" she heard her father's voice boom when Travis opened the door.

Travis held the door with one hand and the top side of the frame with the other, effectively blocking the entrance or even the view into the room. "The occupant of this room," he drawled. "Who are you?"

"I'm Ralph Logan, Katherine's father. The desk clerk told me she was in here. I suppose you're her *husband.*" Katie flinched at the way he said the word, as though he didn't believe she was really married.

"I suppose I am," Travis replied, his quiet tone firm with certainty.

Oh, boy.

Reluctantly, Katie slid off the bed and went to join Travis. She should have known she wouldn't be lucky enough to avoid her parents until the hearing.

She slid under Travis's arm and confronted them. Her father stood in front, his gaze dark and glowering. He never seemed to change. For as long as she could remember, he'd been bald, red-faced and portly. He'd seemed middle-aged when she was a child, and he still appeared no older.

The same applied to her mother. Though she'd seen her mother's hair turn from dark brown to steel gray, her severe expression never changed. Maybe she pulled her hair back in its bun so tightly, she stretched the wrinkles out of her rigid face.

"Hi," Katie said, unable to bring herself to call them *Mother* and *Father.*

"Katherine, this has gone far enough," her father declared. "I have no intention of allowing you to make a spectacle of our entire family in the courtroom."

Katie's lips tightened as she searched for the words to counter this absurd announcement. In her fantasies, she always came up with perfect rebuttals, replies that had her father sputtering ineffectually. In reality, he could still make her feel like a helpless child.

Travis wrapped his arm around her shoulders and drew her against him. "And I have no intention of allowing you to attack my wife. If you can't talk to her in a civil tone, then you can't talk to her."

Her father gave Travis a fleeting, haughty glance, then turned his attention back to her. "Katie, come out here. I want to speak to you *alone.*"

"Nope, that's not civil." Travis pulled her back and closed the door in her father's astonished face.

Chapter Four

John felt a shiver pass through Katie's body as he wrapped both arms around her.

"It's okay, sweetheart," he assured her. If he'd ever had any doubts about the accuracy of Katie's story, those doubts had vanished with the appearance of her parents. She hadn't exaggerated when she stated her case; no child should have to grow up in the care of those people.

She pushed back from him, her hands on his chest. "I need to..." She hesitated, biting her lip. Then her jaw set and her lips firmed as if to deny the moment of vulnerability he'd glimpsed. "I need to get ready for the custody hearing. We don't want to be late."

The custody hearing. He lifted a hand to his forehead as a memory teased at the periphery of his mind, taunting him with its nearness, then swirled away.

He found he was gritting his teeth in the effort to reach that elusive memory. But it was no use. The harder he tried, the blanker his mind became. The sensation was maddening and a little frightening. When this hearing was over, he probably should give in and see a doctor.

He watched Katie across the room as she pulled lacy underwear from her suitcase and took down a dark blue suit and white blouse, both with price tags still dangling, then headed for the bathroom. He couldn't suppress a smile at the sight. Very likely the first conservative suit she'd ever owned, judging from what little he knew of her so far.

He had to give her credit. She'd turned her life upside down to try to save her nephew from the childhood she'd lived through.

The childhood she'd lived through. He sank onto the bed, letting that thought penetrate. It went a long way toward explaining some of her unusual behavior. No wonder Katie had a few hang-ups with the creatures from the black lagoon for parents.

But she was strong. She'd overcome a lot already. Maybe she still had a few problems, but she was his wife now, and he'd take care of her, help her overcome her fears, show her she could trust him. Last night, he'd glimpsed the passion her parents had managed to subdue but not kill. Not his Katie. She was a survivor.

He heard the groan of the old faucets as she turned on the shower, and his mind filled with a mental picture of her slim body with rivulets of water streaming down smooth skin. Damn! He ought to be able to remember a wife like that.

Well, he might not be able to find his love for her in his memory, but he could see why he had fallen in love with her. She was a hell of a woman. Good-looking, sexy, fun to talk to and a totally honorable person.

John held Katie's clammy hand as they sat on the bench in the hall outside the courtroom. Her attorney droned on in a boring, repetitive briefing of appropriate courtroom behavior and what they could expect. Brad Fletcher was a small, nervous, nondescript young lawyer, not the experienced, cold-blooded shark John suspected they needed.

"Have you seen the social worker's report?" Katie interrupted the monologue.

"Yes. Yes, of course. It's favorable. She feels you could provide a loving, stable home for Nathan. You and your..." His gaze fell to John's too-short pants and inappropriate athletic shoes. "Your husband."

Why couldn't he have at least borrowed clothes that fit?

"Well, then that should settle it," John said firmly. "We're acceptable guardians. What's the problem?"

"My father and mother. They're the problem."

Fletcher ran a small hand through his thinning brown hair. "The Logans already have temporary custody. We have to prove not only that you and Katie would be good parents, but that you'd be better parents than they would. And Ralph Logan is very well respected in this town."

John didn't like the way Fletcher sounded when he talked about Logan. Almost reverent. Definitely frightened. Katie might be paying his fee, but John suspected the man wasn't really working on her behalf.

"Will the judge let Katie testify about the kind of parents they were to her?"

"Of course. He'll listen to her, but that doesn't mean he'll believe everything she says. Mr. Logan is—"

"Yeah, yeah. I know. 'Very well respected.' And he and the judge probably play golf together. Don't you worry, sweetheart. If we have to, we'll appeal this case to the Supreme Court."

John felt Katie stiffen beside him. He looked up to see Ralph and Nadine Logan coming down the wide hallway, accompanied by another man carrying a polished black leather briefcase. Their lawyer, no doubt. Twice Fletcher's size with dark, piercing eyes and a square jaw, he'd eat the little man alive. A young boy in a black suit held Nadine's hand, his steps dragging as she pulled him along.

"Nathan," Katie whispered, rising.

The boy must have heard. He looked in her direction, and a smile split his solemn face. "Aunt Katie!"

She crossed the space separating them and knelt beside him, wrapping her arms around him.

"I've missed you so much, Aunt Katie. Where have you been?"

Nathan tried to cling to her, but his grandmother kept a tight hold on his hand.

"Come along, Nathan," Ralph Logan said firmly.

As if the order had been physical, Nathan ceased his struggles to hold on to Katie and let his grandmother lead him. However, the pleading look he cast over his shoulder would have melted the polar ice cap.

John went to Katie and, clasping her shoulders, gently lifted her to her feet. "It's going to be okay, baby. I promise." She didn't appear comforted. She gave him a frantic look, then pulled away.

"It's almost time. Can we go into the courtroom now?" she asked. She stood with her back to him, and her words were brisk, hiding the pain he knew she was feeling.

"Sure, I guess so," Fletcher agreed, picking up his scuffed brown briefcase.

Close behind her, John reached around to pull open the heavy old door. She halted, seemingly reluctant to go in. John didn't blame her. The courtroom was big and solemn and intimidating. Rows of dark wooden benches led up to the judge's bench that loomed over the entire room.

She turned and looked up at him. "You see how important this is, don't you?"

It was, he thought, an odd question, but Katie was under a lot of stress. "Of course I do."

"Whatever it takes, I *have* to get custody of Nathan."

"I understand that."

"The situation calls for extreme measures."

"Katie, are you trying to tell me something?"

She hesitated for a brief instant, barely long enough for him to notice. "Only how desperate I am."

"You're not planning to do something crazy, are you?" Maybe she wasn't as responsible as he'd thought.

She considered that for a moment. "No. I'm not *planning* to do anything crazy." She marched determinedly into the courtroom, head high, slim back erect.

She was terrific. No doubt about that.

But her brief hesitation when he'd asked her if she was trying to tell him something and the slight emphasis on the word *planning* in her last comment had left him wondering. What could she possibly have done that she didn't want to tell him? Organized a kidnapping in case the hearing didn't go her way? He was pretty sure she wasn't carrying a gun, so that excluded shooting her way out.

He was being silly. Katie would never do anything *that* desperate. *Would she?* What did he really know about her?

John ordered that thought from his mind. He'd married her. Surely he could trust his own judgment...even if he couldn't remember it.

Katie made her way down the aisle and took a seat on the unyielding wood of a front-row seat. Suddenly she realized she was alone. Travis wasn't with her.

For an instant, panic and despair swept over her. She turned around to see him coming down the middle aisle and was astonished at the relief she felt.

Man! The stress was really beginning to tell. Why should she be upset if Travis wasn't beside her, then relieved to know he was joining her? She must be starting to believe her own pretense. Travis was nobody to her. She certainly didn't need his help. Having Travis here was simply her way of turning a drawback into an asset.

Though she couldn't deny that things were getting totally out of control. Travis believed her story so completely, he'd lost his private detective persona. He was being incredibly nice, incredibly concerned, the perfect husband. Still, she knew better than to believe her own fabrications and depend on him the way she would have depended on her friend, the real John. Any minute now, Travis Rider could regain his memory, and...

She shuddered.

That was the crux of the matter. She had no idea what would happen when his memory returned. She couldn't decide whether he'd strangle her, denounce her loudly and publicly, maybe even right here in the courtroom, or whether she would have had time to convince him of her side of things. Her impromptu scheme had a few drawbacks.

Well, she hadn't had any choice. She couldn't have let Travis go on to testify against her. She'd done what had to be done, and she could and would go on from there.

She lifted her chin resolutely just as Travis took the seat beside her and Brad Fletcher took the other side. If Travis decided to strangle her, she was a goner. Fletcher would be totally ineffectual.

The Fletcher part of this scenario wasn't very promising, either. She'd hired the only other firm in town besides the one her father used, and they'd sent Brad. She couldn't help but wonder if the partners of the two firms had conspired against her, both of them working for her father.

She ordered herself not to think that way. This hearing could have only one outcome.

Travis draped his arm around her shoulder. It was a comforting and comfortable gesture, and she caught herself leaning toward him, enjoying his touch, wanting to be closer.

What was the matter with her? She'd apparently slipped a cog somewhere. She ought to lean away, make some effort to keep things from getting more inextricably complicated with every passing minute.

But her body refused to obey the commands of her brain. It liked being just where it was.

And maybe that wasn't all bad, she consoled herself. If she moved away, he might become suspicious, and that might trigger something in his brain and bring everything back. As long as she was doomed to sit next to him, she might as well relax and enjoy it.

Anyway, it would soon be over. After the custody hearing, she'd check out of that motel.

And he'd check out with her. Oops. Slight problem there. They'd driven here together, in her car. He'd have to ride back to Dallas with her.

She could handle that. Somehow. Then once they were home, even if he hadn't regained his memory, she'd tell him the truth.

And then?

She couldn't think about that now. One crisis at a time.

"Katie!"

"Oh, Mary!" Katie leaped to her feet and embraced the small blond woman, then turned to the tall man with her and flung her arms around him, too. "Paul! It's so good to see you both!"

"It's good to see you, too, Katie," Mary said. "Even if the circumstances aren't what we would have liked." She turned to Travis. "This must be your new husband. I'm Mary Anderson, and this is my husband, Paul. We're Nathan's other grandparents. Darryl was our son."

Travis stood and smiled, extending his hand. "Pleased to meet you. Yes, I'm John Dunn, Katie's husband."

Oh, jeez! She'd never intended to involve these two wonderful people in her scheme. If John—the real John—had come with her, she'd planned to tell them the truth, but that was pretty much impossible now.

"Nathan's in the hall," Mary said. "Did you get to see him?"

Katie grimaced. "*See* is the right word. That's all I got to do. They dragged him away. Oh, Mary, he doesn't look like himself at all. He's got to be miserable in that monkey suit, and they cut off all his hair. I'm surprised they didn't shave the top of his head so he'd look like his grandfather."

Mary sighed. "I know. We've only managed to get visitation a couple of times, and he's always very subdued. It breaks my heart." Her voice caught on the last words, and her eyes misted. "I'm sorry," she said, blinking rapidly.

Katie patted her hand, feeling her own eyes grow damp. "I know. You lost your son, I lost my sister, and we both lost Nathan."

Mary nodded. "It's been rough. I don't think we'll be able to accept Darryl's and Becky's deaths until we can be sure Nathan's happy. That poor child has to deal not only with losing his parents but also being stuck with those two."

"Not for long," Travis said as he slid his arm around Katie's waist. There it came again, that crazy impulse to lean against him. Somehow her body seemed to fit his. An unfortunate physical characteristic that didn't make this situation any easier. "We're not going to leave here without that little boy," he finished.

Paul Anderson clapped a hand on Travis's shoulder. "Good for you, son. We'll be here to help all we can. Becky and our Darryl would have wanted Katie to raise Nathan. We intend to tell that to the judge."

The door at the back of the room opened again, and Katie looked over to see her parents and Nathan come in, accompanied by a fortyish, matronly woman dressed in a gray suit. Nathan was still firmly restrained by his grandmother, but his head moved as he surveyed the room. When his gaze met Katie's, he smiled and lifted his free hand waist-high in a tentative wave.

The woman moved on to the table in front of the benches on the side opposite Katie and spread papers in front of her.

"That's Liz Benton, the court's advocate for Nathan," Mary whispered.

Katie's parents sat in the row across from her, positioning Nathan on the far side. All she could see of her nephew was his short legs in the sharply creased black slacks, his toes barely touching the dark carpet.

"All rise." Katie jumped at the loud intrusion of the bailiff's voice. Mary squeezed her hand, then moved hurriedly to the row behind them. "This court is now in session, the Honorable Cranston Grimes presiding. All those who have business before this court, please come forward and you will be heard."

This was it. This was the time she'd waited for, planned for, worried about, looked forward to and dreaded. Katie was glad to be able to sit down. Her legs suddenly felt like overcooked, cold spaghetti.

She looked again at Nathan's feet, then up to her parents. The Logans sat staring straight ahead, their expressions as rigid and unrevealing as they'd always been.

So intent was her focus, she didn't hear the preliminaries and was startled when her father's lawyer stood.

"Your Honor, we request a continuance. My client has been unable to contact a material witness."

A continuance? More time for Nathan to be tortured by his grandparents? More time for Travis to regain his memory? No, that wasn't a good idea. She jabbed Brad Fletcher with her elbow. "Object!" she whispered.

"Uh, I object, Your Honor," he said, rising clumsily, a file sliding from his lap to the floor.

The black-robed judge peered through wire-framed glasses, looking from one attorney to the other, his expression every bit as unrevealing as her parents'. Travis was right. Her father doubtless played golf with Cranston Grimes. This was a small town with only one country club. They would probably have dinner tonight. While she had dinner with her father's detective.

She had to squelch a hysterical giggle at that thought.

"What witness would that be, Mr. Winters?" the judge asked.

"Your Honor, my client has in his employ a licensed private detective in Dallas." Travis's sharp intake of breath sent a cold arrow down Katie's spine. *Had he suddenly remembered?* Her heart seemed to clench around her ribs, never mind that such an action was physically impossible.

"This detective," Winters continued, "has promised to have some very illuminating information concerning Ms. Logan's—excuse me, Mrs. *Dunn's*—" he turned his piercing gaze on her briefly "—qualifications as a parent." As she'd hoped would happen, the man in the motel had been busy. "In the interests of determining the best legal guardian for the minor child, we request a twenty-four-hour continuance to give my client time to contact Travis Rider."

Travis's thigh against hers on the hard bench was deceptively warm and reassuring. Katie held her breath, waiting for him to leap up and announce his identity. When it didn't happen, she looked warily from the corner of her eye. Travis was squinting as though in pain, rubbing his forehead with the fingers of one hand.

"Ms. Benton, do you have any objections to a continuance?" Judge Grimes asked the advocate.

"No objections, Your Honor. We are willing to do whatever will serve the best interests of the minor child."

"Very well, then. Request for continuance is granted." He banged his gavel, and Katie jumped.

"No, wait!" She sprang to her feet.

The judge glared at her.

"Sit down," her lawyer whispered.

"Mr. Fletcher, does your client have a problem with the court's ruling?" the judge asked.

A problem. That was the quintessential understatement.

Rapidly scrolling through her mental list of problems, Katie discarded having to spend another night with Travis in that little motel room and in that little bed, running the risk that Travis might recover his memory at any time, and considered the fact that she hadn't seen Nathan in three months and, of course, the harm that even another day with her parents would do to Nathan.

"Your Honor, I haven't been permitted visitation with my nephew during the entire three-month period since his parents' deaths," she said, choosing the only problem she felt the judge might listen to. "This isn't fair to either him or me. This matter needs to be resolved as soon as possible."

"Mrs. Dunn, you were granted visitation. This court is not responsible for your failure to exercise your rights." He lifted his gavel again.

"Maybe the court isn't responsible, but my father damned sure is."

He cracked the gavel. "Swearing is not permitted in my courtroom."

"I apologize. Your Honor." She was beginning to sound a little obsequious even to herself, but she'd *Your Honor* him to death if it meant rescuing Nathan.

He nodded curtly. "Mr. Logan had no responsibility to bring the minor child to Dallas so you could exercise your visitation rights. Your expectation that he do so was unacceptable. Perhaps since you're here now, you can manage to take advantage of the opportunity."

Katie felt her mouth sag open in shock. She tried to speak, to deny the ridiculous charge, but her vocal cords were paralyzed with the shock of her father's latest duplicity.

Travis stood beside her, making her paralysis even more complete. Was he going to expose her? Was the whole thing about to blow up in her face?

"Your Honor, my wife is trying to say that you've been given incorrect facts. She came to Hillsdale to visit her nephew, but her father refused to let her see him. Just now outside the courtroom, he wouldn't let her have even a few minutes with Nathan."

She should have been relieved that he hadn't recovered his memory and hadn't identified himself as the missing witness. And she was. But in addition to feeling guilty for deceiving him when he was being so nice, she knew that every good thing he did for her, everything he said in her favor would turn into a black mark against her when he remembered.

"Is this true, Ra—Mr. Logan?"

"Of course not. She never made any attempt to see Nathan."

"I certainly did," Katie exclaimed in outrage.

"We can back her up on that," Paul Anderson said from behind her. "She came by our house when her father ran her off."

"Stay out of this, Anderson. Don't lie for her." Ralph Logan was speaking to Paul, but glaring at Katie.

To his credit, the judge didn't look totally convinced of her father's sincerity, even though his slip of the tongue made it obvious the two were friends. "We'll take that up at the hearing tomorrow. In the meantime, I'm sure Mr. Logan will be happy to permit visitation today. You can work out the details in the hall."

"Thank you, Your Honor," Katie said and looked again at her father to see how he was taking this turn of events.

His expression hadn't changed. She should have anticipated that.

Travis took her arm, and they walked together out of the courtroom. When they emerged into the hallway, Travis stopped and turned around. "Where's that damned Fletcher?" he growled.

"I'm sure he's right behind us."

But she wasn't surprised to see Winters emerge from the door next. "Your father doesn't want Nathan to spend the day in a motel room," the lawyer said.

"Therefore, he'd like you to come and visit with him in his home."

"No." The word came out before she even had time to think about it.

Winters compressed his lips irritably. "Surely you can understand that, after all the trauma the child has gone through, his home life should be disrupted as little as possible. He'll be much more comfortable if he's in familiar surroundings rather than being trapped in a motel room or dragged around town."

"He will be in familiar surroundings," Paul Anderson said, pushing through the door behind Winters. "You kids get your luggage out of that motel and come stay with us. You have any problem with Nathan's coming to our house, Winters?"

Katie could tell from the frustrated look on the man's face that he did have a problem with it—or at least he knew his clients would. "I'm sure that will be fine."

"We'll pick him up in two hours," Travis said.

Winters nodded curtly and disappeared back into the courtroom, presumably to deliver the bad news to her parents.

"Thanks, Paul." Travis shook the older man's hand again. "We appreciate the hospitality."

"It's our pleasure," Mary replied. "Katie's always been like our other daughter-in-law. We're delighted to have the both of you. This will give us a chance to get to know you better, John. We want you to feel like one of the family."

That should be interesting, Katie thought in dismay. They could sit around and ask questions of her father's amnesiac detective, and she could continue honing her lying skills by making up answers to those questions. By the time this was over—if it ever was—nobody would be speaking to her.

Oh, what a tangled web!

At least they would be out of that tiny, confining motel room. She didn't think she could have stood another night of such close proximity to Travis.

"We'll put you in Darryl's old room. It's been empty since he and Becky got married."

Darryl's old room. Panic spread over Katie like butter on a hot biscuit.

Travis's hand slid around her waist again and came to rest on her hip, a gesture of intimacy and familiarity. It felt nice. He felt nice. Just when she'd thought things couldn't possibly get any worse.

She could remember Becky giggling about Darryl's old room and how tiny the bed was. That was where, on a weekend when Darryl's parents had been out of town, Nathan had been conceived.

Their old motel room was looking better and better.

"Ready, babe?" Travis asked, and she realized Paul and Mary were walking away.

"Ready?" she squeaked. "Oh, sure. Let's go."

When a person was already in over her head, what difference did another foot of water make?

Chapter Five

Katie slowed the car as they drove up the hill and approached the two-story, square, unadorned white house. It squatted in the middle of an immaculate lawn with perfectly manicured shrubs and one perfectly tidy and symmetrical tree precisely centered.

"That's where I grew up," she announced. She couldn't call it home. It had never been that.

Travis had wanted to drive when they left the motel, but Katie had been able to stop him by reminding him that he had no driver's license. She hadn't wanted him to drive. He was already assuming much too active a role, getting too involved in her predicament. However, now she almost wished she had let him. It took every ounce of her willpower to turn in to the driveway. If she'd been alone, she would probably have gone around the block half a dozen times before she would have been able to force herself to stop.

"Being here give you the willics?" he asked.

"A little," she admitted. In fact, she felt as if a steel band had tightened around her chest. If it weren't for the fact that Nathan was imprisoned inside that house, she'd leave.

"Why don't I go up to the door to get Nathan while you wait here?" Travis offered.

The combination of guilt when Travis was being so kind and irritation at herself for feeling that guilt propelled her out of her state of fear. She yanked on the door handle. "I'll go. You wait here."

He didn't. She wasn't surprised to hear his door slamming in echo of her own.

As he moved beside her along the sidewalk, he wrapped his arm comfortingly around her waist, and for the briefest instant, she wanted to absorb that comfort, revel in it and claim it for her own.

But it wasn't hers. It was obtained under false pretenses. If Travis were himself, right this minute they'd be in the courtroom and he'd be ripping her to shreds instead of walking beside her.

She walked faster, trying to get away from him. But, of course, his legs were much longer than hers. He had no trouble keeping up. She had the sudden sensation of being trapped between Travis and her father. One nudge in Travis's brain cells, and that would be only too true.

She stepped up to the door and jabbed the bell.

Her father appeared almost instantly as if he'd been waiting. "I'll expect Nathan back by 9:00. That's his bedtime. Maintaining a routine is very important to a young child. Don't let him have any sugar or caffeine. It makes him too excitable."

Katie nodded, biting her lip to keep from reminding her father that she was only too familiar with his list of dos and don'ts.

Finally he stepped back and Nathan walked stiffly through the door. He no longer wore the suit but had on khaki pants and a white cotton shirt. Not play clothes for the rough-and-tumble boy she remembered.

"Hi," he said almost timidly. Ralph and Nadine Logan could do that to a kid.

"Hi yourself. I've missed you!" She stooped to wrap her arms around him, her gaze flicking over and away from her father's disapproving face.

Nathan immediately threw his arms around her neck, and she straightened, raising the boy off his feet. "My gosh, you've grown so big, I can hardly lift you! You been sipping the Miracle-Gro when nobody was looking?"

Nathan giggled. "No!"

She heard the door close as she set Nathan on the ground, and the bands around her chest loosened. She could breathe freely again.

Almost.

From the corner of her eye, she caught a glimpse of Travis.

"Nathan," she said, turning to face Travis, "this is—" She hesitated, the words sticking in her throat. Just as she couldn't tell Paul and Mary the truth, neither could she tell Nathan.

"I'm your Uncle John," Travis said, extending a hand to Nathan. "Your Aunt Katie and I are married, and she's told me all about you. I'm glad to finally get to meet you."

Technically speaking, she hadn't lied to Nathan. Travis had, and Travis was the enemy.

The rationalization didn't make her feel much better.

"Okay," she said, "let's get this show on the road. How about first we go downtown and find you some jeans and a T-shirt so you won't get in trouble for messing up your clothes, then we go eat a greasy pizza and wash it down with a gallon of cola?"

"All right!" Nathan agreed with a big grin.

Travis smiled approvingly.

They were just one big, happy family.

Except for that time bomb ticking inside Travis's head.

"How broke are we?" John asked. He and Katie were waiting outside the dressing room in Hillsdale's only department store while Nathan tried on faded jeans and a T-shirt bearing the picture of some rock group. John didn't think he'd ever heard of the group, but he'd probably have to say the same thing about his favorite preaccident singer.

"Broke?" She looked up at him, her expression startled and confused.

"You said I borrowed Fred's suit because I didn't have one. I was just wondering if we had enough money for me to get a suit that covers my wrists and ankles for the hearing tomorrow."

"Yes, yes, of course we do. We're not broke. The suits are right over there. They're not top quality, but you can probably find one that will fit better than Fred's." She pointed to the corner of the store where he'd already noticed them hanging. "Here." She fumbled in her purse. "Take this credit card."

Oh, yeah. His missing wallet.

Reluctantly he took Katie's card. He supposed it all came out of the same bank account. After all, they were married.

But somehow it didn't feel right.

On the way to the suits, he stopped at the men's underwear section. The only briefs they had were tiger-striped, but at least they wouldn't bunch up the way these boxer shorts did, especially under the jeans he'd changed back into. Was it possible that crack on the head had affected his taste in underwear?

Or had he borrowed Fred's underwear as well as his suit?

Absentmindedly, he picked up a package of the tiger briefs and bounced it in his hand.

Borrowing underwear didn't make any sense. He could accept the story that, as a resident just starting his career, still paying off school loans, he didn't have a decent suit. But he found it hard to believe he didn't have underwear. The ones he'd been wearing last night seemed relatively new—unfaded, no holes. Surely he owned more than one decent pair.

Something else besides the suit and shoes didn't fit. The scars on his stomach that he somehow knew were knife wounds, the searing way Katie had responded to his kisses, then refused to touch him the rest of the night—but more than that, something in his gut just didn't feel right.

He glanced across the store to look at Katie. Nathan had come out of the dressing room and looked like a different kid. Not only because of the change of clothes, but even from this distance, John could see the difference in Nathan. He stood straighter than he had at the trial. He was smiling and talking enthusiastically with his aunt.

He felt a little ashamed of his suspicions. How could he doubt a woman like Katie? Even setting aside his prejudice as her husband, no one could deny that she was a kind, caring person.

He turned away and headed for the suits.

After the promised pizza stuffing and cola downing, Katie drove to the Andersons' house.

"What a difference!" John exclaimed. He hadn't meant to say anything; the words had just slipped out. Though both this house and the Logans' house were white, two-story structures, they had no other similarities. This one had green shutters, a porch with lawn furniture, an open front door, several big trees in the yard and a riot of colorful flowers exploding everywhere.

"Yeah," Katie and Nathan agreed in unison, an act which set both of them to giggling... again. They'd been doing that a lot, every giggle reassuring John that all his doubts would be resolved when he got his memory back. Nothing covert could possibly be going on here.

Mary Anderson came out the door followed by her husband, and Nathan scrambled from the car to run to them.

John cupped his hand around the back of Katie's neck. "You're doing the right thing, babe," he said.

She gave him an odd look. A guilty look? Guilty of what? Before he could be sure, she slid out of the car to follow Nathan.

He strode up the walk behind her. The boy bounced up and down excitedly as he talked to his grandparents and waited for Katie.

As he watched, an almost palpable wistfulness flooded over John. He grasped at the sensation, but it slipped away and he was left clutching only a hazy recollection of wanting a home and family. Not a lot to go on. He supposed that was pretty much a universal desire.

Still, it was a start on regaining his memory.

Paul Anderson hastened down the walk to meet him. "Let's get your bags, John." He clapped him heartily on the shoulder. "We've got Darryl's room all fixed up for you and Katie." They turned back toward the car, and Paul lowered his voice. "Ralph give you any trouble picking up Nathan?"

"A lot of orders, but no trouble."

Paul laughed. "He's good at giving orders. Fortunately, Katie's just as good at ignoring them. You got yourself quite a woman there."

"Yes, sir," John agreed, not only because it was the polite thing to do, but also because he was pretty sure it was true. Give or take a few irregularities.

Mary and Nathan went inside, but Katie remained watching the two men as they headed to the car. She didn't like the idea of Travis being alone with Paul. What if Paul asked him some questions he couldn't answer? He'd been so adamant the night before about keeping his "problem" a secret, and she was certainly in favor of that. She'd just as soon keep the whole thing quiet—at least until the inevitable moment when it would blow up in her face.

"Aunt Katie, can we play baseball?" Nathan burst through the door with a scruffy ball in one hand and a glove on the other.

"In a minute, sweetie. Let's go help Granddad and, uh, Uncle John with the bags."

"Okay."

But Katie could tell it wasn't really okay. The poor kid had been through an awful lot these past few months. He'd lost his parents, been trapped with cold, demanding grandparents, and now that he was back with his Aunt Katie, she was asking him to share her with a stranger.

She mussed his hair, ran a hand through it from the back of his neck to the front, then trailed a finger down his forehead to his nose.

He giggled and shook his head. "Quit!"

"Come on, kiddo. This won't take long. We'll be out in the yard playing ball before you know it." Travis and Paul were halfway back, but she started down the walk toward them anyway. "Need some help?"

Paul grinned. "We've got it under control. This husband of yours has got a strong back. You work out, John?"

"Yes, he does," Katie interjected before Travis even had time to worry about his answer. It was pretty safe to assume he worked out. His chest had certainly felt solid and muscular when she'd explored it in the dark last night, not to mention its width and well-defined muscles when she'd seen it in all its naked glory this morning. She swallowed hard and pulled herself back to the present from that particular tantalizing memory.

The present was pretty tantalizing, too, she realized. His arms as he carried the bags were corded and bulging, and his black T-shirt delineated every hill and valley of that chest she was becoming increasingly familiar with. He didn't get that kind of muscle development from holding a tape recorder outside decent people's windows.

Travis gave her a quick, conspiratorial wink and a smile as she met him and turned to walk beside him. For a moment, she thought he might sense her admiration of his physical endowments. *Don't be silly,* she chided herself. *He's only thanking you for covering his rear.*

"Hey, Nathan," he said, looking around her at the boy, "is that a baseball you've got there?"

"Yeah. Do you like to play baseball?"

"I sure do."

Katie cringed at the decisive way he answered without the slightest hesitation. How did he know he liked to play baseball? If he knew that, what else did he know?

When he continued to talk about the game with Nathan, she breathed a sigh of relief. If he'd remembered anything significant, he'd have dropped the suitcases, pinned her arms behind her back and forced her to confess to the world what she'd done to him with her little iron skillet.

Travis seemed quite comfortable and at ease as Mary joined them, and the five of them climbed the stairs to Darryl's old bedroom. Nathan was rapidly relaxing as he answered Travis's questions about his school and friends. Mary and Paul were obviously pleased to have everybody there. Katie was the only one whose nerves were as frayed as an old electric cord left in an attic for years and chewed on by mice.

They reached the top of the stairs, and Paul led them to an open door.

"This was my son's room," he said, setting the bags he carried inside the door. His smile slipped just a notch and his voice cracked ever so slightly. Mary moved to his side and put an arm around him. Katie went to his other side and embraced him. "It's time we opened it up," Paul said, his voice husky as he returned her hug, "and I can't think of anyone I'd rather see staying in here than you two."

"He's right," Mary agreed quietly. "Darryl and Becky always hoped Katie would find someone to be happy with. I know, wherever they are, they're thrilled that you'll be together in Darryl's old room."

Major guilt trip.

Katie moved away from Paul and Mary and walked woodenly into the small room.

It's okay, she told herself. *Becky and Darryl would approve of what I'm doing for their son.* This was an unorthodox situation and called for unorthodox remedies.

She looked around. Posters of sports heroes covered the walls and a bookshelf in one corner held a few books, a portable radio and other odds and ends left over from a teenage boy's life.

The white-painted iron bed frame with its faded Indian blanket was, as Becky had described it, "very cozy." Almost an antique, it dated from a time when people and beds were smaller. And one side of that tiny bed was shoved against the wall. No escape there.

The motel room where they'd spent last night seemed spacious and roomy in retrospect.

"Well," Paul was saying, "I guess you kids will want to get settled in. Nathan, why don't you come downstairs with Granddad and we'll toss that ball around. Your daddy used to play with that very ball when he was your age."

Nathan hesitated, looking from his grandfather to her. Undoubtedly he didn't want to leave any of the people he'd been separated from for so long. And she didn't need to be isolated with Travis any longer than necessary.

"We'll go with you. We don't need to get settled," she said hastily, and was pleased to see Nathan's expression lift.

That gave her a perfectly legitimate reason not to have to be alone with Travis and that little bitty bed. It was, she could already tell, going to be another sleepless night.

Maybe it was the heat. Maybe it was so much pizza. Maybe it was lack of sleep catching up with her. Or maybe it was anticipation of the mounting number and intensity of the time bombs ticking around her.

Whatever the cause, after about an hour of backyard baseball, Katie was hot, tired and tense. She was playing all the bases and outfield while Nathan pitched, Paul batted, Travis caught and Mary lounged in the shade drinking a glass of iced tea.

Travis gave a complicated series of finger signs, and the pitcher broke into giggles.

"That doesn't mean anything," Nathan protested, laughing.

"Sure it does! It means throw the ball at a twenty-six-and-a-half-degree angle so when Paul hits it, it'll go through the window of the house next door, and that's an automatic out."

Nathan laughed again and rolled his eyes at Travis's silliness.

Within a few minutes after they had begun to play ball in the backyard, Nathan had bonded with his "Uncle John."

Of course, Paul and Mary would welcome any husband of hers, real or pretend, with open arms, but they seemed to genuinely like Travis. *Everybody* liked her new husband. Nobody was going to be happy when she told them the truth. Especially Nathan, who'd already lost too many people from his young life. Several hundred more beads of perspiration popped out on her forehead at the thought.

The three of them might just decide to keep Travis and divorce her.

A *crack* splintered the air. Paul dropped the bat and began to run. The ball soared high overhead.

Katie ran backward. "I got it! I got it!" She jumped and reached, caught the ball and fell. Pain shot through her ankle, hurting so intensely it momentarily took her breath away.

"Are you okay?" Travis called.

"I'm fine." *Probably slipped in the lake of perspiration this situation was generating,* she thought, pushing herself up with one hand while hanging on to the ball with the other. "And you're *out,* Paul Anderson! *Argh!*" Again the pain shot through her ankle, tearing the shriek from her throat as she crumpled back to the grass.

"Katie!" Travis charged across the yard toward her.

Nathan, nearer to start with, reached her first, followed closely by Travis, Mary and Paul. They all looked so worried, for a moment she felt overwhelmed by so much concern and caring. Except one-fourth of that concern and caring stemmed from false pretenses.

"Aunt Katie, did you hurt yourself?"

"I just twisted my ankle. No big deal." She tried to rise, more cautiously this time, wincing and falling back when the pain increased.

"Let me see that." Mary knelt beside her, lifted her foot gingerly and started to untie her shoe. Then with the laces loosened, she turned to Travis. "What am I doing? We have a doctor in the family now." With a smile, she offered Katie's foot to Travis.

Travis's gaze met hers for a brief, shocked instant as he tentatively accepted her foot.

"John isn't that kind of doctor," Katie hastily interjected. "He doesn't know anything about feet." A private detective probably wouldn't be able to tell if her leg were broken unless it lay in two pieces.

Travis busied himself removing her shoe and sock. His big hands were amazingly gentle, caressing as they touched her skin. Actually, he seemed to know quite a lot about feet, though she was pretty sure none of his knowledge had anything to do with the medical field.

"I can't find anything broken," he said, his fingers tantalizing as they glided around her ankle. He looked up at her, his hazel eyes glowing with a curious mixture of helplessness and desire. A curiously compelling mixture.

He cupped her heel in the palm of his hand, his fingers spreading over both sides of her ankle, his thumb moving across her arch, the action sending electric tingles to the farthest outposts of her body. Oh, my. She'd never before known a foot could be so sensitive. So sensual.

She had to stop herself from suggesting that he keep on checking. She wouldn't have minded if he'd continued to do whatever he was doing for another hour or so.

But every touch was another brick in the wall that would eventually collapse on her.

She wiggled her toes. "See? It's not broken." She'd heard somewhere that was a good sign. "Already it doesn't hurt as much as it used to. It's practically all better. Can we get up now?"

Travis laid her foot on the grass, then stood and reached down, lifting her easily. "Lean on me," he ordered, and she thought she detected a hint of huskiness in his voice. Had the contact affected him the way it had affected her?

She didn't want to lean on him, didn't want to touch those wide, hard shoulders, or feel herself pulled against that muscular chest that just kept intruding into her life. Well, actually, she wanted to do all those things. Wanted to real bad. And that was the right description. *Real bad.* Dangerous. Suicidal. Dumb.

His strong arm pulling her against his body didn't give her much choice. She wrapped one arm around his neck and held on as she limped toward the house.

You're trapped, Katie Logan, she told herself. *Pretend it's just another adventure. Relax and enjoy the ride until it's over.*

But she couldn't. Okay, so she was enjoying the feel of her body pressed against Travis's. So her adrenaline and who knew what other chemicals were running rampant through her body. She might be enjoying this latest death-defying adventure, but she damn sure wasn't relaxed about it!

Mary held the door open, and Katie, assisted by Travis, crossed the room to the big old sofa. She moved slowly, probably more slowly than was absolutely necessary. If she was going to go skydiving, she might as well enjoy the ride down as long as possible, she reasoned. By now she could see the ground zooming up to meet her.

Travis didn't seem to be rushing her, either. If anything, he held her back. It was nice to know, she supposed, that he was on the same wild trip as she...except he was part of the earth surging upward to end her airborne journey.

He helped her get situated on the sofa, then took the ice pack Mary brought and wrapped it around her ankle. His fingers lingered when the task was completed, trailing miniature forest fires up her leg, all the way to the knee.

With a smoldering look of regret, he ended his ministrations and stood.

Oh, that look. Oh, that little bed waiting upstairs with night looming only a few hours away. Was it her imagination or had the sun begun to sink in fast-forward?

"Better?" Travis asked.

Was she reading a double entendre into that question?

"Better," she said, looking at her foot instead of him and trying to make her voice sound perfectly normal. "My ankle's fine. I really don't need this ice." She wanted to kick the pack away, stand and run around the room and work off some of that excess energy Travis's touch had generated, those chemicals that were still charging around in her body.

On the other hand, she probably shouldn't take any chances with her ankle. She didn't want to be handicapped in case she needed to run away very fast when Travis found out the truth.

Nathan sat down beside her, cuddling close, and it dawned on her that he hadn't said a word since her accident. She turned to him and rumpled his hair. His face was pale, his eyes wide. He looked scared.

"What a baby I am," she said, searching for some way to reassure him he wasn't going to lose somebody he cared for yet not embarrass him in front of the others. "There's really no need for all this fuss. I'll bet you don't have to be carried off the playing field every time you get hurt a little bit."

"Nah." A proud grin curled the corners of his mouth. "One time I got a bloody nose, but it didn't bleed very long. Made a real mess on my shirt. Grandmother Logan got pretty mad."

"Yeah," Katie agreed. "She got pretty mad at me when I got ketchup or mustard or ice cream or…well, about every time I ate anything, half of it ended up on my clothes."

He laughed, and she relaxed. Later she'd have another talk with him and explain that everything was going to work out. And it would. Somehow she'd see to that. After everything she'd already done, she couldn't imagine there were any lengths to which she wouldn't go.

"So what kind of a doctor are you, John?" Mary asked, returning from the kitchen with a tray of iced teas.

Travis took a glass and compressed his lips into a frustrated line.

"Ob-gyn," Katie blurted. That should keep them from asking him to perform any medical services.

Travis's eyes widened in astonishment.

Chapter Six

An ob-gyn.

From the back seat of the car, John watched the shifting evening shadows in Katie's hair as she drove to her father's house to return Nathan.

He still couldn't quite reconcile himself to his chosen occupation. Learning he was a doctor had been a pretty big shock, but an ob-gyn? Even though he still had recovered only vague impressions of his life and no specific memories, it just didn't seem to fit.

But Katie was his wife. Surely she knew what kind of doctor he was.

Unless she'd lied for his benefit to cover up the fact that he couldn't remember how to treat a sprained ankle.

He'd have to talk to her about it later.

There were a lot of things he needed to talk to her about later.

She turned in to the familiar driveway. The summer twilight wrapped around the harsh lines of the house without any softening effect. John hated the idea of sending Nathan back in there.

In the front seat, Katie and Nathan sat motionless, staring straight ahead. He placed a hand on each of their shoulders. "It's time," he said quietly.

Katie sighed. "I know." She turned to Nathan. "Come on, kiddo. You can do one more night."

Nathan looked up at her. "You promise? Just one more night?" His words of hope were tainted with doubt.

Katie looked down at her lap, drew in a deep breath, then lifted her head. She gave John a glance he couldn't read in the gathering darkness. "I promise I'll do everything in my power to see that it's only one more night. But if it does take more time than that, you have to swear you'll be strong and wait for me and not give up."

Eyes downcast, Nathan nodded.

"Swear." Katie held up her right hand, little finger extended.

Nathan hooked his little finger around hers. "I swear." The boy turned in the seat and extended his other hand to John.

John linked his finger with Nathan's. "I swear we'll get you out of this, Nathan," he promised.

As the three of them walked up to the front door of the Logans' house, John experienced the sinking, sad sensation in the pit of Nathan's stomach as if it were his own. He felt acutely the loss of love, the fear of going through that door and into that life.

The door in question opened and Ralph Logan appeared, a menacing silhouette against the backdrop of interior lights. For an instant, the features of a face seemed to appear on that dark shape, a face that didn't belong to Ralph.

"Uncle John, are you coming?"

John realized he'd stopped several feet away and was gaping at the man in the doorway, trying to focus on the face that wasn't there, had never been there. Katie stared at him, her eyes big and dark.

"Yes, I'm coming. I was just thinking about something." He smiled at Katie and shrugged, trying to let her know he was all right.

But he wasn't.

Nathan lifted his arms to give him a goodbye hug. John wanted to hold on to the boy, to grab him and run as far away from that house as possible. Instead, he hugged him and reluctantly sent him on. With a strangely hollow feeling, he watched the child's small frame as the house swallowed him, as the door closed behind him, shutting him off from the rest of the world.

"What's the matter?" Katie's voice held a slight quiver.

Wordlessly he turned to her, wrapped his arms around her and pulled her close, seeking and, he hoped, giving comfort. She wasn't just his wife; she was also someone who'd survived the situation they'd delivered Nathan into. But as much as he'd have liked to stand there all night with her slim body pressed to his, he wanted just as badly to get away from the Logan house.

"Let's go," he said and led her to the car. For once he was grateful she was driving. "I think I remembered something," he said as she backed down the driveway.

She stopped the car in the street to change gears. "What?" she asked, not looking at him, not proceeding onward down the street.

Almost as if she feared what he might remember.

"I thought I was feeling Nathan's distress at having to go back to his grandparents, but I think part of it was remembering my own."

"You lived with your grandparents?" She sounded surprised.

"I don't know. Did I?"

"What did you remember?" she asked, ignoring his question.

"Just impressions. The threat of being left with somebody I didn't want to stay with. Somebody I *dreaded* staying with. Damn!" He slammed his fist onto the dashboard. "Why can't I remember? It's like everything I know about myself is lurking right behind me, and if I could turn around fast enough, I'd catch it."

She took his fist in hers, wrapping both warm hands around it. "I have to tell you something," she said, her voice uncharacteristically solemn. "What you asked me about whether or not you lived with your grandparents—"

"No kid should have to feel like that. You're right, Katie. Whatever it takes, we have to rescue Nathan."

Katie nodded, dropped his hand, faced forward again and nudged the gas.

"So what were you going to say?" he asked. "Were my grandparents like your parents? Did I live with them?"

She cut the next corner a little sharply, tires squealing in protest. "Not that I know of," she said firmly.

"Did you mean what you said about doing whatever it takes to get custody of Nathan?"

She'd changed the subject, skittering away from talk of his past as she always did. For the moment, he decided, he'd let her get away with it. They'd be arriving back at the Andersons' in a few minutes. There wasn't time now to do much probing, to try to get his questions answered. Later, when they were closeted together in that small bedroom, when she couldn't get away, then they were going to talk.

He didn't for a minute doubt her sincerity or even that he could have loved her enough to marry her, but she wasn't coming up with the right answers. In fact, she wasn't coming up with any answers.

"Of course I meant it," he replied. "It's easy to see we'd make the best parents for him. Besides, I know that something similar happened to me when I was his age. Even if I can't recall it right now, I know it's made me determined that the same thing shouldn't happen to other kids."

"Thank you." She breathed the words, and he wasn't sure if she were thanking him or God.

"The first thing we need to do," he said, "is to get a different lawyer. Brad Fetch-it is either on your dad's payroll or he's terrified of him. He's worse than not having a lawyer."

"We don't have a lot of choice. There're two firms in town. My father's lawyer is the senior partner of one, and Brad's the junior associate of the other."

"Then we go to another town. We file our own motion to get a change of venue."

She cast him a quick, surprised glance, then immediately turned her attention back to the road ahead. "What's a change of venue?"

"It's asking the judge to order the case heard in another court because you can't get a fair hearing in the one it's in."

"Oh, that. I already asked Brad. He hemmed and hawed around, but basically the problem is that, since the judge is friends with my father, he's not going to agree to have it changed."

"Yeah, you're probably right. But we still need to go ahead and do it. That way, at least, we'll have it on record, and we can use it in our appeal, if it comes to that. Reversible error."

"Good idea," she said stiffly, gunning the car faster and faster as if she couldn't wait to get back to the Andersons'. He'd like to think it was because she was anxious to be alone with him, but that didn't seem very likely.

"Katie, I know it doesn't sound like much, but I've seen enough courtroom maneuverings to know that it's the little things that count, the technicalities. I—" John stopped in midsentence. "How do I know all that legal stuff? What kind of courtroom maneuverings could I have possibly seen? I'm a doctor, an ob-gyn, for crying out loud. How often do I go to court?"

But he knew he did go to court, as surely as he knew he'd once been in as bad a living situation as Nathan, as surely as he knew he had the scar of a knife wound in his gut.

Katie didn't answer him. He wasn't surprised.

Katie burst through the door of the Andersons' house as though it were the door out of the labyrinth. Which wasn't too far off, she reflected.

Paul and Mary looked up, calm and smiling, as she came in. Paul was stretched out in a big recliner and

Mary sat on the sofa while the television flashed in the background. The scene was so tranquil, so normal, she wanted to rush in and bury herself in it.

Dispelling that hope, Travis, her own personal Minotaur, followed right behind her. At least for the moment he didn't dare ask her any more questions she couldn't answer. She'd come so close to admitting the truth, but when he'd affirmed that they had to do whatever was necessary to rescue Nathan, she'd taken that as a sign. Becky's guardian angel was again letting her know she was on the right track in spite of the rumbling of the freight train close behind her.

"How'd it go?" Paul asked, snapping off the television with the remote control.

"Nathan didn't want to leave. I felt like a traitor forcing him to do it." Katie flopped onto the sofa beside Mary and lifted her injured ankle onto the coffee table.

"I know," Mary agreed. "The two times he's been allowed to come over here, I felt the same way taking him back."

Travis knelt beside her and lifted her foot. Oh boy. Here came the magic fingers again. Seemed like she was always trying to get away from him for one reason or another.

"I think it's swollen more since you've been on it," he pronounced, his fingertips gliding over the sensitive skin.

"I'll go get some ice," Mary volunteered.

"Why don't you bring us something to drink while you're at it, honey," Paul requested.

"You got it." Mary winked at him and left the room.

"You kids don't know how much good you're doing for everybody," Paul said. "Nathan needs you the most, but we're sure glad you're here. Losing Darryl and Becky and then not getting to see Nathan just about did Mary in. I was worried about her for a while."

"And what about her husband?" Katie asked. "How are you handling all this?"

"It hasn't been easy for me, either. We've both spent way too much time fretting about the past. Having you two and Nathan here has brought us into the present. John, we're proud to have you as a part of the family."

Paul's words brought a happy smile to Katie's lips even as they heated up the smoldering caldron of guilt she'd been dipping into all day. She didn't like deceiving these people she loved. She'd never meant to. If the real John had been able to make it, they'd all be sitting around laughing about her little deception. But John wasn't here, and this deceit was a bad side effect she hadn't counted on.

Even if she'd had time to think about it and consider all the ramifications, she'd never have believed Paul and Mary and Nathan would like Travis, would actually approve of her "marriage." She'd never have believed the man prowling around outside her house could be so likable.

"Thank you, Paul," the likable jerk replied in his most charming voice. "I'm pleased to be included in your family."

Mary returned with the ice pack, a bottle of wine and four glasses. She handed the ice pack to Travis, set the glasses on the table and began to pour. "We've been saving this for a special occasion, and I can't think of anything more special than Katie's marriage."

Okay, one more ladle of guilt. Just pour it over the top of my head, thank you.

Travis accepted his wine and sat next to her on the sofa. Katie lifted her glass along with everyone else while Paul toasted the "happy couple."

"May you be even happier twenty-five years from now than you are tonight," Mary added.

That part shouldn't be too difficult.

As the others sipped from their glasses, Katie sniffed hers dubiously. Did wine drunk under such false pretenses cause instant death or madness or something even worse—like uncontrollable truth telling?

At this point, only an hour or so away from being trapped all night in that tiny room with Travis, what did it matter? She tossed down half the glass.

"You know, we're a little miffed at you, Katie," Mary said, sinking onto the sofa beside her. "You never said a word about John. We heard about him this morning from Rita—our neighbor who dedicates her life to gossip, John—and she heard about him from the motel manager."

Not bad enough she had to worry about coping with Travis's questions tonight. Suddenly she was surrounded. She wiped a sweaty palm on her denim shorts. "Well, it all happened so suddenly, and so much was going on with Nathan and all."

"I told Mary that was probably what happened," Paul said. "I always knew if Katie ever got married, somebody would have to come along and sweep her off her feet before she had time to think about it."

Travis draped an arm around Katie's shoulders and looked into her eyes, his gaze probing. The combination of thrills generated by his arm and chills generated by his gaze would have been enough to send her into cardiac arrest—if she hadn't already been in shock.

"Why's that, Paul?" he asked.

Paul smiled at her affectionately. "Katie was always too busy to think about tying herself down to one person. After she got away from Ralph and Nadine, she didn't want anybody having control over her life. I'm sure she told you how she ran all over the world—the Amazon, Europe, Africa, Mexico. A new adventure every time we saw her. But we always said the right person could change all that."

Katie felt so small, she feared she might sink into the crack between the sofa cushions. In fact, that wouldn't be such a bad idea.

Travis squeezed her shoulder, a familiar, affectionate gesture.

Little did Paul know this could be her greatest adventure yet. Certainly the riskiest. To him, she probably seemed to be perched on the edge of his sofa. In reality, she was perched on the edge of disaster, quietly sipping wine with, and greatly enjoying the embrace of, her father's hired gun, a rotten detective out to ruin her.

A rotten detective out to ruin her. She mentally repeated the last sentiment, hoping to squelch some of the enjoyment. It didn't work.

"We've never had the slightest hesitation supporting Katie's becoming Nathan's guardian," Mary affirmed, "even when we figured he'd have a nontraditional upbringing." Travis tensed, sucking in a quick breath. "And that would have been just fine," Mary continued, patting Katie's arm. "But we're thrilled with your new life-style. I have to confess, when Rita first called me this morning, I told Paul I was a little worried you might have jumped into this marriage just to help you get custody of Nathan."

"But I told her that wasn't possible," Paul said. "Nothing but a love so strong she couldn't help herself could make Katie get married. And the minute we saw you two together, we knew that was right." Paul beamed at the two of them.

Katie shifted back and forth on the sofa, trying desperately to disappear down that crack.

It was just after eleven when Travis lovingly helped her up the stairs, cautioning her not to reinjure her ankle. It ought to be more like three in the morning if time operated on an emotional basis instead of a physical one. The last couple of hours had seemed interminable while she tried to dance around the probing questions of Paul and Mary. When they'd suggested going up to bed, for one fleeting millisecond, she'd felt relief. That was how long it had taken for her to remember who was going up to bed with her.

Katie walked into Darryl's old room with Travis still supporting her. He turned and closed the door behind them. This house probably had the only bedroom in the city with a lock that sounded as if it belonged to a torture chamber in a fourteenth-century dungeon.

"They're great people," Travis said, sitting down on the side of the bed to pull off his shoes.

"I know." She stood in the middle of the floor. Some middle. He could reach her in one grab.

"They really care about you." He plunked one shoe onto the floor.

"I know." She sank onto the bed next to him. What difference did it make? She'd soon be lying on that bed beside him.

The other shoe joined the first. That should free him up so he could take off his pants now.

"I think they like me, too," he said.

"I know."

He stood.

Here it came. The undressing scene. The more-than-you-ever-wanted-to-see-of-Travis-Rider scene. Except she did want to see it. Again. That was the really scary part. Rather than looking the other way, her gaze followed his every move.

But he didn't lift his shirt over his head, exposing that chest she figured she knew every hair of by now. He didn't grasp the zipper of his jeans, unzip them and display those wild briefs he'd bought today.

Instead, he sank, fully clothed, to his knees in front of her.

"How's your ankle, babe?" he asked, lifting her foot and untying her shoe.

Oh, this could be even worse than watching him strip if he started that foot stuff again. Now that they were alone. Just her and him and The Bed.

She yanked her foot away. "Fine. It doesn't hurt at all. How's your head?"

"Fine." He touched his head and grinned up at her. "It only hurts when I do this, so I try to avoid doing this." He sat on the bed again. Very close to her. "So are you up to a little conversation?"

"Actually, I'm pretty tired. It's been a long day." She gave a fake yawn that turned into a real one. *And a long night the night before.*

He smiled a smile that rode the border between wicked and happy. "So you're ready to go to bed?" His voice echoed that smile and set up answering echoes inside her. She closed her ears to the call of the sirens. This was no time to lose her head. Or anything else.

"Oh, I guess I'm not all *that* tired."

"Me, neither." Yeah, she could have guessed that.

"So, what did you want to talk about?"

"I'm starting to get bits and pieces of memory back, but I think it's time you told me a little more about myself, about us."

Yeah, she could have guessed that, too.

Chapter Seven

"Are you sure you can do this? Make a normal life for Nathan, I mean."

Katie opened her mouth to protest in outrage, but he lifted an admonitory hand. "I know you love him, and I know you'd do anything for him, including changing your life. But what if it doesn't work? What if raising a kid and living in the same house in the same town with the same job year after year makes you feel trapped? What if you want your old life-style back? You can't just pick up a child and cart him around the world while you're chasing your dreams."

Travis's words evoked a burst of bittersweet vindication. The man who'd stood beside her in court, fought her battle against her parents, worried about her when she twisted her ankle... the man who could turn her blood to molten lava was changing back into her father's hired gun. Well, hired tape recorder anyway.

Worse, he was turning into her father, criticizing her decisions and her life-style, coming up with his own agenda for what she should and shouldn't do. He was acting the way she'd always feared a husband would—and he wasn't even a real husband.

She rose from the bed and walked across the room, where she stood with her back against the wall, as far away from him as she could get. "I am perfectly capable of giving Nathan a good, loving home. If you don't think I can, just what would you suggest we do? Leave Nathan with my parents?"

"I'm not saying that." He leaned forward, holding one hand out, palm upward, in a conciliatory manner.

"Then what are you saying?"

"I don't know." He slapped his thigh. "Damn it, Katie, I don't know very much of anything right now."

Katie folded her arms. "As I recall, it's only been a couple of hours since you said we'd be better parents than my mother and father."

"I still think that. It's just that..." His brow furrowed as if he was trying hard to concentrate. To focus on returning memories?

Katie dropped her hands behind her and pressed her palms to the wall, bracing herself physically and emotionally. "Just what?"

He frowned. "When Paul was talking about how, uh, *diverse* your life used to be, I had a vision of a little kid being dragged around, changing schools every few months, leaving all his friends, never having any stability in his life."

Yeah, he was starting to remember. That sounded like something her father would have told him.

"There are a lot of worse things that can happen to a kid," she said, tilting her chin defiantly. "Like my parents, for instance."

He nodded, rubbing the back of his neck. "I know. I guess the truth is I'm not just worried about Nathan. I'm a little worried about us, you and me, in spite of what Paul said. For some reason I'm getting an uneasy feeling."

That was quite enough to give her an uneasy feeling, too.

"What do you mean?"

He shook his head again and compressed his lips. "This is so damned frustrating. My whole life is playing hide-and-seek with me. I get this sense of dread that you're going to go tripping all over the country. The picture won't quite focus, but it's like I can see you doing that and making me crazy. Did I ever try to stop you from doing all those things before you decided to settle down for Nathan?"

Tripping all over the country and making him crazy. "No, of course you didn't try to stop me. You didn't even know me. We didn't meet until I'd—"

His attitude made her reluctant to complete the thought about her change in life-style, as if in making that change she had somehow acquiesced to his desires, admitted he and her father were right, once again relinquished control of her life.

Well, she hadn't. She'd done it for Nathan, not because anybody else expected it or wanted it. "Until I'd settled down," she said firmly. "Anyway, you don't have any right to judge the way I live. Lived."

He strode over to her and pulled her into his arms.

Amazing. This jerk's body felt just like the nice guy's.

She held herself stiffly, arms at her sides, refusing to allow her treacherous body to mold to his the way it kept wanting to.

"Katie, sweetheart, I'm not arguing with you," he said, his warm breath stirring her hair. "I'm just trying to understand, to get my own thoughts clear. A doctor's search for knowledge."

Or a detective's snooping, prying nosiness.

"Which reminds me of another question I need answered." He leaned back slightly and tilted up her chin so she had to look into his eyes. The movement pressed his pelvis against hers. Between the sensations that action caused and her concern about what he was going to say next, looking into those piercing eyes wasn't high on her list of ways to relax.

"What?" she managed to croak, though she certainly wasn't anxious to hear the question. Even if she could force herself to lie while pinned by his gaze, she suspected his nearness had her too confused to concoct a coherent story.

"I'm having a really hard time seeing myself as an ob-gyn. Did you just make that up so I wouldn't have to practice doctoring skills that I can't remember?"

Katie blinked, replaying Travis's words in her mind. She'd been ready for him to confront her, demand to know about his childhood, his favorite foods, why she refused to sleep with him. She was astonished she'd gotten off so easily and laughed unexpectedly in relief. Travis's head tilted to the side for a moment, then he began to laugh, too.

"It's not true, is it?" he accused. "You did make it up."

The questions were getting easier and easier. She nodded. "I made it up."

"I'm not an ob-gyn."

She shook her head.

"You told everybody I was because you knew they'd never ask me to perform that kind of medical service."

She nodded. "It worked." He laughed again, hugged her, whirled her around and around, and they ended up on the bed, still giggling.

Leaning over her, he traced her lips with one finger. "You're an original, Katie." He replaced his finger with his lips.

Somewhere inside her head, warning signs flashed a bright red, but red had always been Katie's favorite color. She closed her eyes and returned the silky, demanding kiss. Her arms entwined around his neck, this action the only logical one to keep her from falling off both the tiny bed and that lopsided world she seemed to be teetering on.

Travis's mouth moved on hers, warm and soft. It was such a nice mouth when it wasn't asking questions she didn't want to answer.

His hand slid lazily, enticingly across her stomach, his fingers closing over her ribs, kneading and caressing, then traveling slowly down her shorts to her naked thigh. Oh, my. The foot business paled beside this. With those hands, Travis should have been a doctor. A surgeon.

Those flashing red signs finally made their way into her consciousness.

Travis wasn't a surgeon. He was a private detective. Her father's private detective and a controlling man. And he was starting to get his memory back. Kissing him wasn't a good idea at all, no matter how good it felt.

She dragged her arms away from his neck, placed her palms on his chest and, reluctantly, pushed.

With a groan, Travis pulled away from her, then flopped over to sit on the side of the bed. He dug all ten fingers into his hair and squeezed his head.

Katie sat cross-legged in the middle of the blanket, holding her breath to see what memories the head squeezing might draw forth.

He turned to her, frustration in every line of his face. "Katie, I want some answers *now.*"

Things had seemed a whole lot better when he'd been kissing her. For a brief, enticing moment, she considered kissing him again, cutting off his questions. In fact, if they made love, maybe he'd fall asleep afterward and completely forget about asking questions.

Or maybe they'd make love all night.

Shut up, Katie, she admonished herself. Those were insane thoughts. Even she couldn't do something that dangerous, that self-destructive—that tempting.

"Are we really married?"

"You saw the license I gave the motel manager."

"Then why don't we make love? You want me as much as I want you, so what's the problem?"

"The problem? Uh, well, the problem. The problem's birth control. It's in your missing wallet."

His gaze was dubious. "Then why didn't you mention it earlier? I'll bet even the merchants in Hillsdale sell them. Besides, we have other options."

She'd just as soon he hadn't added that last. Against her will, her mind filled with kaleidoscopic images of some of those "options."

"Travis, I—"

Katie realized her mistake the moment the word was out of her mouth. Travis frowned as if in deep thought.

"Travis Rider," she plunged on, trying to stop his thought process before it went too far. "My father's detective, he's got me all upset. The idea of somebody following me around, snooping on me. What kind of slimy sleazeball would do that? I tell you, *John,* I have so much on my mind with this hearing, I'm totally stressed out. Can't we wait until everything's over to discuss all this?"

He threw his hands into the air. "Okay, fine. But there's no reason we can't talk about other things. Why did I borrow clothes that don't fit? Why did I have white boxer shorts in my suitcase when I was wearing black briefs? Where did I get this?" He lifted his shirt to expose the upper part of a jagged scar that disappeared into the waistband of his blue jeans.

The scar both frightened and attracted her. She wanted to run her fingers over it, trace it all the way down.

"What do I know about guns and courtrooms and change of venue?" he continued, fortunately drawing her mind away from its crooked path. "How does that fit in with being a doctor? And how old am I? Aren't I a little old to be a resident?"

Guns. That was a great piece of information to come back to him, she thought sarcastically. He'd know how to murder her if he chose to. But that, together with the scar and the courtroom stuff, inspired her.

Even as the fiction unfolded in her mind, Katie hesitated, a little uneasy. She'd been trying not to go too far afield in creating the fictional John, but her original idea of having an opportunity to plead her case had grown a little out of hand. She didn't know how to stop now, how to back out without making the damage worse than ever, without jeopardizing Nathan's future.

"Katie?"

She took a deep breath. "You're thirty-five. This is your second career. You were a police officer, and you wounded so many people, you decided to go back to school and become a doctor and heal them instead."

A pretty masterful creation, she thought, watching his expression go from curious to thoughtful. "A police officer," he repeated, and she could tell he believed her.

She'd done a good job. So why did she feel all icky inside? One more lie, big or small, shouldn't bother her at this point. She'd probably set some kind of a record for fabrications over the past couple of days.

There was absolutely no reason for her to feel guilty about lying to The Enemy. Okay, so Travis *seemed* to be on her side and *seemed* to be helping her—most of the time.

It was all pretend, all part of her creativity. He'd change back to the real Travis Rider as soon as he regained his memory.

"That feels right," he said quietly, almost to himself. "I vaguely remember working on a case, trying to find evidence against—"

"That was a long time ago," she said hastily, interrupting his thought process before he got to the part about the person he was trying to find evidence against—probably her. "You've been to medical school since then. Of course, you were pretty bright.

You finished fast." Maybe a compliment would divert him from the path her story had set him on.

"How fast? How many years was I in medical school?"

Katie frantically tried to recall how long the real John had gone to medical school. She'd been in Europe when he started. Or was it Mexico?

"I don't know. That was before we met. And, as we've already discussed, we haven't known each other very long."

"How long?"

"Look, I know you want all the answers, but not tonight. I have just got to get some sleep." She slid off the bed, threw open her bag, yanked out her nightshirt and dashed down the hall to the bathroom.

It was awfully tempting to curl up in the bathtub and spend the night there. But that not only sounded uncomfortable, it would give Travis more ammunition for his questions. She waited a few extra minutes. Maybe by the time she got back, he'd be asleep. He hadn't slept any more last night than she had.

When she opened the door to the bedroom, he was stretched out on the bed wearing nothing but the mat of hair on his chest, that frightening, alluring scar and those wild, tiger-striped briefs. And he was quite obviously not even close to being asleep.

As she walked into the room, his eyes raked over her, making her feel sexy, as though she was wearing red silk lingerie rather than a long, cotton nightshirt.

"I have to tell you something," she blurted.

"Okay. Tell me."

Her mind went blank. The rest of her body was talking loud and clear, so loud it drowned out whatever thought she'd had. "Tell you what?"

"Katie, you're the one who said you had something to tell me. Never mind. It's late. Why don't you come to bed?" He rolled onto his side as though making room for her next to him. Against that chest and that scar and those briefs.

"I lied." Had she really admitted that? What the heck could she say as a follow-up?

His gaze became wary. "About what?"

"Us. We, uh, we did get married because of Nathan. With all your school loans, you needed a place to live, and I needed a husband."

A look of self-loathing replaced the desire on his face. "I married you for a place to live? What kind of a man am I?"

A thoroughly rotten excuse for a human being, she wanted to say. *The kind of a man who spies on and plots against a woman who's just trying to do the right thing.* She had him down now. She ought to kick him in the teeth.

But the words wouldn't come out. She was getting too involved in her own lies. She actually felt sorry for Travis.

"You did it for me," she heard herself saying even as she wondered where the words came from. She launched herself onto the bed beside him and wrapped her arms around him.

He pulled away from her. "It wasn't the way Paul said at all. We didn't get married because we were so madly in love that you trusted me and didn't worry about losing control of your life."

He stated it as a fact, not as a question, so she didn't respond.

This latest lie was the closest she'd come to the truth with Travis. It should take care of a lot of the complications that had arisen from her deception. Travis would no longer believe he loved her. He'd stop acting like the adoring husband. He'd stop assuming he should have some control over her life. He'd stop trying to consummate their marriage. She ought to feel better about things, relieved that some of the pressure was off, at least for the moment.

Strange, she thought, as she lay beside Travis, inches and miles away from him, how large that bed had suddenly become.

John felt a little numb as he followed Katie into the courtroom the next morning. Her revelation of the night before was proving to be as hard to deal with as his amnesia.

He and Katie weren't in love. Their marriage was a business deal. It made sense, explained a lot of things, like the cheap wedding ring, the nervous way she acted every time he got close to her and her reluctance to make love.

But it didn't explain the feeling of loss her news gave him. How could he lose something he'd never had?

Liz Benton already sat at her table. She smiled tightly and nodded as they came in. But, John told himself, at least she smiled. Surely that was a good sign.

He and Katie filed over to the same bench as yesterday. Paul and Mary sat behind them. John was grateful for their presence. He suspected he and Katie were going to need all the help they could get.

Katie reached for his hand, and he looked up to see the Logans coming in with their attorney and Nathan. John squeezed her hand reassuringly. Maybe they'd entered into this situation as a business deal, but it seemed to him that things weren't turning out that way. His feelings for her definitely weren't businesslike, and he could tell she felt the same way even if she wouldn't admit it.

Paul's words came back to him—he'd feared, because of the way her parents had treated her, Katie would never tie herself down and give up her independence. So while she had married him, it was only for the purpose of gaining custody of Nathan. He had no claims on her.

That was why she panicked every time he touched her. She was attracted to him just as he was to her, but she didn't dare admit it, didn't dare let down her guard. She didn't trust her own emotions.

Well, they were married and he was living with her. He'd have plenty of time to change her mind. When he returned to normal, they were going to have to renegotiate this deal.

The Logans took their seats in the row across, and Ralph turned toward them with a cold, triumphant look. John didn't like that one little bit. He felt Katie tense beside him.

"Don't let him bluff you," he whispered.

"My father doesn't bluff." Her hand in his was small and cold.

"It's going to be all right, sweetheart."

Her eyes widened at the endearment. It had slipped out so naturally, echoing the way he felt. But they could talk about that later, when the stress of this hearing was over. For the moment, he chose not to explain or to change the way he expressed himself.

"Where the devil is that imitation attorney of ours?"

Katie nodded toward the back of the courtroom. Brad Fletcher came through the door, head bowed, seeming to study the floor as he made his way down the aisle, not lifting his eyes even when he reached them.

John casually stretched his legs out to prevent the attorney from going to the far side and sitting next to Katie.

"Morning," John said. "I saved you a seat right here."

"Good morning." Fletcher sat down and opened up his briefcase. Still he didn't look at them.

"What's the good word?" John asked. He had an uncomfortable feeling there wasn't one.

Fletcher closed the briefcase without taking anything out of it. His small, pale fingers fumbled nervously with the latches, and his gaze, when he finally raised his eyes, was uncertain. "I think they have that missing witness, that detective."

"They do?" Katie sounded astonished. "Are you sure?" John made a mental note of her surprised reaction. Did she know something about the detective?

"No, I'm not sure," Fletcher said, "but they have something."

"What?" John demanded.

"Have you seen him?" Katie asked.

"No, I haven't seen him. How do I know what they have? I'm not working with them."

John wasn't so sure about that. "You're entitled to discovery of their evidence."

"I don't have time to file a motion for discovery. We'll know in a few minutes anyway."

John glared at him until the attorney looked away. "I'm warning you, Fletcher, if you sell us out, I'll have your—" He broke off, deciding it probably wasn't a good idea to threaten a lawyer with bodily injury in a courtroom. "I'll have your license," he concluded.

Fletcher lifted his hands in a gesture of surrender. "I'm doing the best I can."

"That's probably the truth," John grumbled.

Beside him, Katie gave a brief, nervous laugh.

The bailiff walked in and began his spiel.

When the judge was seated, the Logans' attorney stood. Katie's hand clutched his convulsively. He hadn't realized she was so strong.

"Your Honor, we've had a new development in this case." He cast them a dark, enigmatic glance.

"Go on, Mr. Winters," the judge urged.

"As you know, my client's primary witness, a private detective named Travis Rider, failed to show for the hearing yesterday."

"And I don't believe I see him here today, Mr. Winters," Judge Grimes remarked. "Does this mean you're still unprepared to proceed?"

The judge sounded irritated. It was the first encouraging sign so far.

"I'm afraid there's a little more to it than that." Again he glanced in their direction. "My client has been unable to locate Mr. Rider."

"I'm sorry your client hired someone he couldn't trust, but this court can't wait forever. Everyone else has made an appearance for the second day in a row." He swept a hand to include Liz Benton as well as Katie and him.

"I understand, Your Honor, but I believe the circumstances justify another continuance. No one can find Mr. Rider. He's disappeared."

"Again, Mr. Winters, this court cannot take responsibility for the unreliable behavior of your witness."

"Your Honor, the possibility exists that Travis Rider was the victim of foul play."

Katie sucked in her breath and dropped his hand.

"When my client checked with Mr. Rider's office yesterday morning after we left here," Winters continued, "his secretary just said he was out. But yesterday afternoon she admitted she hadn't seen or heard from him since the day before. His secretary checked his apartment, and neither he nor his car was there. He had messages on his answering machine from the day before." Winters again turned his gaze to Katie and John. "His secretary contacted the police, and they should begin investigating his disappearance today. The last time Mr. Rider was seen, he was on his way to Mrs. Dunn's house."

Chapter Eight

The police?

Katie reached again for Travis's hand, then jerked back as she realized how absurd that would be, seeking comfort from the man she'd—well, whatever *foul play* the police might deem she'd done to him.

Without moving his head, Judge Grimes shifted his gaze from Winters to her, glaring over his glasses. Katie forced herself to meet his eyes even though she felt sure her guilt must be blatantly obvious to everybody, especially to a judge accustomed to dealing with criminals.

"Very well, Mr. Winters, this court will grant one more continuance, but this case will be heard tomorrow whether or not you're able to locate your witness."

Katie sucked in a deep breath of relief. One more day. Now if only Travis didn't get his memory back until after the hearing. And when he did get it back, he remembered how certain he'd been that she should have custody of Nathan. And if only she could keep her head straight about this whole thing and stop wanting to rush into his arms for reassurance.

Travis rose, taking her arm and urging her up along with him when she would have preferred to remain seated and as unobtrusive as possible. "Your Honor, we request that we be allowed visitation with Nathan again today."

"They had him all day yesterday," Winters protested. "The minor child needs to maintain as normal a schedule as possible. Two days in a row away from his home would be too upsetting."

The judge opened his mouth to speak, probably to side with his golfing buddy.

"My father refused to let me see him for three months," Katie protested, her fear of being connected to Travis's disappearance dissolving in her desperate need to help Nathan.

"Your Honor, we've already explained that Mrs. Dunn refused to come to Hillsdale to visit the minor child—"

"That's not true!"

Winters pointed an accusatory finger in her direction. "That woman is a liar and possibly even a kidnapper or a murderer."

Katie gasped, her hand flying to her mouth.

The judge banged his gavel.

"That's enough, Counselor. One more accusation against this woman, and I'll hold you in contempt. Visitation is ordered again today, and the court will hear this case tomorrow whether or not your mysterious detective shows up." He banged his gavel again, decisively.

Katie's knees went weak with shock. The judge had actually sided with her. Winters had pushed him too far. Maybe they'd be able to get a fair hearing after all.

Travis's arm slid around her waist, and she sagged against him gratefully.

Mary leaned forward and patted her arm. "You see, everything's going to be fine. We'll meet you at the house."

Katie nodded. "Yes. We'll be there as soon as we get Nathan."

Outside the courtroom, her parents and Winters were hurrying away with Nathan in tow.

"Logan!" Travis called, and to her surprise, her father stopped and looked back. "Why don't we take Nathan with us now instead of having to drive all the way over to your house?"

Nathan's face lit up, though she noticed he made an effort not to smile. Her father glanced at Winters, who gave a barely discernible shrug.

"I think not," her father said. "He needs to change clothes. I don't want him ruining his good suit."

"No problem. We bought him jeans and a T-shirt yesterday."

Ralph Logan's chest expanded and his nostrils flared. "You can pick him up at my house."

Travis crossed his arms and rocked slightly backward on his heels. "Makes a lot more sense to take him with us now."

The two men glared at each other for several silent seconds. Katie wouldn't have put any bets on who the winner might be. Travis's strength both amazed and frightened her, but she knew only too well how willful her father could be.

To her astonishment, her father broke first.

His lip curled disdainfully. He lifted a hand. "Take him." He turned and walked away with his wife on one side and his lawyer on the other.

Nathan charged down the hall toward them, arms spread wide to embrace both of them.

One part of Katie wanted to grab Travis and hug him and laugh and do a little dance right there in the middle of the courthouse. Travis had stood up to her father and defeated him. That same part of her was excruciatingly happy and proud of her extraordinary husband.

But the rest of her knew that that part of her was totally nuts.

"What did you do with that detective?"

Katie jumped at the unexpected question. For a split second, she thought Travis had asked it, and her spirits sank at his doubting her—even though she was guilty.

But the question had come from Brad Fletcher, who was standing behind them. He'd been so quiet throughout the entire proceedings, she'd completely forgotten about him.

"What do you mean, what did she do with him?" Travis demanded, his voice heavy with warning.

Fletcher shrugged. "Hey, I'm her lawyer. Anything she tells me is confidential. I don't really think she killed him. Probably bought him off, didn't you?"

In one quick motion, Travis released Nathan, grabbed Fletcher's tie with one hand and doubled the other hand into a fist.

Fletcher's eyes popped open like those of a fish and his face paled.

Travis turned him loose, shoved him away and relaxed his fist. "If you were my size, I'd punch you in that mealy mouth of yours. I'm warning you, if you ever say one more thing like that about my wife, I'll forget how small you are, and you can forget about your front teeth."

Fletcher smiled nervously. "I was only... I didn't mean... I'm her lawyer. I need to know what's going on." He edged away, then turned and practically ran down the hall.

Katie stretched up to plant a kiss on Travis's cheek. "You were wonderful," she said. "My hero." *My enemy. My kidnap victim.* This whole situation was getting more and more complicated by the minute.

Travis beamed happily, proudly and—no, it couldn't be. He couldn't be looking at her lovingly.

She'd told him they hadn't married for love. She'd tried to make it very clear their relationship was strictly a business deal. He couldn't still believe they cared about each other.

Of course, the way she'd just acted could possibly be construed as caring. She'd have to be more careful, control her impetuosity, avoid giving the wrong idea.

"Okay, folks," Travis said, "let's get moving."

"Can we have pizza again today?" Nathan asked.

Travis winked at her over the top of the boy's head. "You didn't tell me we'd be eating pizza every day after this boy comes to live with us."

Katie and Nathan giggled. "There are worse things in life," she said, "than eating pizza every day."

And she'd managed to cram a substantial number of those "worse things" into the past few days, starting with whacking Travis over the head with her iron skillet. That almost certainly constituted assault. Bringing him across a state line was, she suspected, kidnapping. Or did that only apply for immoral purposes? On the other hand, letting him think he was her husband might rank right up there with those other immoral purposes.

The three of them walked down the wide hallway together. The perfect family.

The worst of her list of bad things, she realized as she watched Nathan and Travis laughing, was how attached she'd become to her kidnappee—in his amnesiac state. As soon as he regained his memory and returned to being a private detective with a knife wound in his gut and a bad habit of snooping, she'd lose this fantasy husband she'd created.

The afternoon was windy. Perfect weather, John had suggested, to fly a kite. Astonishing everyone, including himself, the three of them had succeeded in putting together and getting aloft the biggest kite they'd been able to find.

Nathan stood in the middle of the park, holding the kite as it dipped and soared with the air currents. John walked over to the big elm tree where Katie sat on the grass in the shade drinking a cola.

"Hard to believe this is the same kid I saw that first day in the courthouse," John said, sinking to the ground beside her.

"Mmm," she agreed. "This is the Nathan he used to be before my father got hold of him." Her attention on the boy, she absentmindedly offered John her soda.

For a second, he hesitated, then took the can and drank from it, placing his lips where Katie's had so recently been. The cold liquid quenched his thirst, but the act of drinking after Katie stirred another thirst.

It was an oddly sensual and intimate act, something married people did. And Katie had initiated it without thinking.

She might be fooling herself, but she wasn't fooling him. Somewhere along the line, their relationship had become more to her than a business deal.

He handed the can back to her and watched her drink again, her gaze still on Nathan.

The notion that they had married for mutual convenience was as difficult for him to grasp as his elusive memory. There must have been feelings between Katie and him, even if they had never acknowledged them. Being her husband seemed right. He liked their marriage. And he'd have been willing to swear he loved Katie—even that she loved him in spite of her increasingly bizarre behavior.

"You see why I don't have any problem giving up my old life-style for him?" she continued. "It's worth it. Anyway, we're only talking ten years. When he's grown, he'll leave, and I can go back to being irresponsible."

She looked at him with a teasing grin. As the wind rustled the leaves of the tree above them, sparks of sunshine darted in and out of her hair. The light seemed to come from inside her head rather than from above it. His fingers tingled with the desire to touch her silky, sparkling hair, to feel it lying soft and smooth across his face or his chest while giving off tiny electrical charges.

"Why don't you let your hair grow longer?"

Her smile died. "Because I don't want to."

Her attitude reminded him that he wasn't her real husband. He didn't have the right to ask things like that. "Did your father make you wear your hair long?"

She nodded. "Now I wear my hair however pleases me."

He started to comment, then bit his lip. It was none of his business. She'd made that clear.

The hell with that. They were married. They lived together. He'd make it his business.

"Katie, don't you think it's kind of counterproductive to do things just because they're the opposite of what your father would want? You're free of him now. You shouldn't let him have any influence on your life. You should be doing only what you want."

"That's exactly what I'm doing."

It didn't sound like it to him. It sounded like she was still rebelling, still allowing her father to have an influence over her in the very act of her thwarting him. But her tone of voice and the warning in her eyes told him he was treading on dangerous ground. Since he wasn't even sure of his own ground, he elected to let the subject drop for the moment.

But it bothered him, and he wasn't quite sure why. Something about the way she'd said she only had to give up her old life-style for ten years, then Nathan would be grown and gone, and she could return to her former "irresponsible" life. Maybe because it insinuated that he'd be out of her life then.

No, it was more than that. He feared she'd never be able to settle down and provide a good home for Nathan. A painful picture of her dragging Nathan around the country overwhelmed him.

That wasn't right, he thought, trying to focus on the picture. The woman wasn't Katie. She didn't have golden hair filled with sparks of sunshine. Her hair was dark and long like the night. She—

"Aunt Katie, Uncle John..." Nathan stood in front of them, face flushed, hair sweaty and sticking to his forehead, an enormous grin on his face. His appearance brought John back to the present, his vision fleeing once again into the mists of his memory. "Can I play baseball with my friends over there? I go to school with them. We're in the same grade."

"Of course," Katie said, smiling up at him. "Have a good time. We'll wait right here for you."

"Thanks! Here, Uncle John." He handed over the kite string. "Did you lock the car?" he asked, already hopping backward toward the parking area only a few yards away. "I gotta get my glove."

"The car's open." Katie wrapped her arms around her knees as Nathan darted away. "All kids should be that happy all the time," she said.

"Yeah," John agreed, reeling in the kite. Nathan slammed the car door, then dashed away, glove in hand, to join the group of boys. "Too bad he has to leave his friends." Again he felt the pain as acutely as if it were his own.

"I know," Katie said. "But he's young. He'll make new friends. There's no way I could ever live in this town."

She was right, of course. She didn't need to live in the same town as her painful past. Besides that, her father would never leave her alone if she lived here. Not to mention jobs were harder to find in small towns.

All good, legitimate reasons for her to stay in Dallas. Still, for no good reason, her remark irritated him and stirred something ugly that lurked just below the surface of his mind.

Again, he thought, it had nothing to do with Katie.

Nothing and everything.

He dismissed that vagrant thought. His returning memories couldn't have anything to do with her. She hadn't been in his life long enough to make many of them.

He finished winding the string, then laid the kite against the tree trunk. Lifting the lid of the cooler, he took another soft drink from the crushed ice.

A gust of wind whipped the kite over. John set it up, then shoved the cooler against it. It was a neat kite; they'd fly it again another day.

Popping open his cola, he flopped down beside Katie on the cool grass. As he sat beside his wife under a big tree, the summer breezes soft on his face, the heat of the day held at bay by the shade, watching their nephew play baseball, he didn't know if he'd ever pictured a perfect day, but this had to be close.

It was so perfect, it was almost unreal.

And, of course, it was unreal, a moment of purity snatched from the surrounding chaos. As such, it should be enjoyed to the maximum. He took a deep breath, trying to fill the blanks in his memory with the smell of the heat, the dust from the baseball diamond, the intermittent scent from some hidden flower and, of course, Katie. He leaned closer, wanting to memorize every feature, the pale freckles on her nose, the way the breezes feathered her hair.

As though she felt his scrutiny, she turned toward him, giving him a smile that added to his feeling of serenity.

"Becky and I used to see this park every day on the way to school, but we were never allowed to come here. I miss her," she said, turning away from him, her gaze distant as though she focused not on Nathan across the park but on her sister across time. "I think we were even closer than most sisters since we were all we had." She looked at him again, her expression beguiling, her eyes as blue and open as the Oklahoma sky that spread out all around them.

He ached to touch her, to pull her into his arms, to lose himself totally in the depths of her eyes, to assure her he could and would be everything she desired.

He squeezed his soda can, crushing the flexible aluminum until the drink oozed through the opening in the top. Damn! He had to get back his memory, his life, and straighten out this crazy relationship with Katie.

"Do I have brothers and sisters?" he asked.

Even before Katie responded, he could see the answer in her eyes.

"You don't know," he supplied.

"Not exactly."

He let out a long sigh of frustration. "Katie, you've got to tell me the truth. This not knowing anything is making me crazy. What do you know about me? Had we even met before we got married?"

"Not exactly," she repeated, lowering her gaze to her fingers as she nervously broke off blades of grass.

He muttered a string of oaths. "We got married without ever meeting?"

"You could say that." She kept her gaze on the grass.

He set his drink on the ground and edged closer to her, then tilted up her chin, forcing her to look at him.

"Katie—" Suddenly he no longer knew what he'd intended to say to her. He'd meant to search her eyes for the truth. And maybe that's what he found. The truth of need, of fear, of uncertainty, of desire...

As his face approached hers, he found he could no longer focus on her eyes, so he closed his own. He didn't need to see. His lips found hers unerringly.

She emitted a soft moan, and her arms slid around his neck. He enfolded her in his arms, aware only of his mouth on hers, of losing himself in her. Nothing was real except the places where they touched. Concerns about the custody hearing, his memory loss, the make-believe marriage were all far away. Only the two of them existed, the two of them blending into one.

Her honeysuckle perfume mingled with the green scent of grass and became a part of their kiss, a part of them.

This was no kiss between strangers. This was a joining of souls. He wanted her, all of her. He wanted her body that now clung eagerly to his while her heart pounded in rhythm with his. He wanted to make love to her, to know the ultimate closeness. He wanted to be everything to her. No matter how this marriage had started, he loved her and wanted her for his wife, his real wife.

He pulled away from her, smiling down at her and tracing one finger along the smooth skin of her cheek. Her bright eyes were dusky with passion, with wanting him. His heart swelled with happiness. "Katie," he whispered. "My Katie."

Something hit him from behind, and he whirled around, automatically crouching into a defensive posture. The kite lay on the ground beside him.

"The kite," he said, feeling a little foolish. "I guess it's my police training coming back to haunt me."

Katie sat up, blinking in confusion as if coming out of a trance. "The kite?" she repeated shakily.

"The wind must have tugged it loose. I just set the cooler against it. It wasn't very secure."

Lousy timing, he thought. Or maybe good timing. If not for the interruption, he might have said something to Katie that really should wait until the custody hearing was over. One crisis at a time.

"I'll put this damned thing in the car," he said. *Get up and take a deep breath and move away from Katie until you get your common sense back.*

"Okay." She cleared her throat and stood. "Good idea. I think I'll have another cola."

John watched her reaching into the cooler, her eyes averted from him.

Or maybe it would have been the right time after all. Maybe it was time to stop avoiding the issues.

He strode over to the car and opened the door. Climbing into the front seat, he struggled to shove the kite into the back. It had fitted in just fine when they'd brought it in the box. Nathan had held it on his lap, reading the instructions in excited detail. However, the finished product didn't want to go in. Maybe he should try the trunk, though on this little car, he couldn't imagine it would be large enough for the kite. They might end up flying it out the window as they drove home.

As he tried to take the awkward contraption out again, he realized the blasted thing was stuck. Just what he needed. Another problem. He yanked viciously on one corner, and it came loose, one of the sticks smashing into the glove compartment, which immediately sprang open. Cursing the small car, he backed out, trying not to damage the kite, then reached in to close the glove compartment.

A black leather wallet lay on the opened door.

What was Katie doing with a wallet in her glove compartment? She probably had a perfectly good explanation.

He picked it up and started to put it back inside.

His wallet was missing, and Katie had a wallet in her glove compartment. A coincidence. Didn't mean a thing.

He tried to put it back once more, but his fingers refused to let go of the soft leather.

What was the matter with him? He had no business snooping through her car.

He pulled the wallet out again and stared at it. Something in his gut told him this object held some answers. Something in his former policeman's gut—not his doctor's gut.

He looked back at Katie. She sat on the grass sipping her drink and watching him, the sunlight and shadows dappling her hair and her face. She was his wife, the woman he loved. He had to trust her.

But she wasn't coming up with the right answers.

Still holding it in one hand, he let the wallet fall open. To reveal two credit cards. Both in the name of Travis Rider.

What in heaven's name was Katie doing with Travis Rider's wallet in her glove compartment?

An image flashed into his mind, an image so strong it momentarily obscured the world around him. He was creeping through the bushes outside Katie's house, trying to avoid detection, sneaking up on someone.

The image suddenly disappeared, and he saw that Katie had come over to where he stood. Her eyes, so recently filled with passion, were now filled with fear.

"Travis—" she said.

"Yes," he snapped, holding the wallet out to her. "This is Travis Rider's wallet. Katie, what the hell's going on? Did we catch this detective snooping around our house?"

Her jaw dropped open. "This detective?" she croaked. "Snooping around our house?"

Another image darted through his mind, an image of Katie wielding something in both hands, a weapon of some sort, anger, fear and desperation written all over her face. He closed his eyes and gritted his teeth, trying to hang on to the picture, to see the next frame. But it was a photograph, an instant frozen in time.

"We caught him," he speculated, watching her intently for clues to see how close he was getting to the truth. People always gave themselves away by some small sign—a tic, averting their eyes, becoming flushed. He knew all the signs. "We caught this detective in the bushes outside your house," he went on. "I wasn't chasing your cat that night. I was chasing him. That's how I got hurt."

Her eyes grew bigger and bigger, the panic in them wilder and wilder with every word. He was on the right path.

"He hit me," he continued, "and you hit him. That's what happened, isn't it?"

She stared at him wordlessly.

He dropped the kite and the wallet and grabbed her shoulders. "Katie, answer me! I've got to know what happened. Did you kill Travis Rider? Did I? That's why Fred went outside through the kitchen and came in through the living room, isn't it? He wasn't putting up the ladder. He was hiding the body."

"No!" She pulled away from him and stood. "Travis Rider isn't dead. He's alive. I promise."

It was true, then. In spite of his speculations, in spite of the evidence in front of his face, he hadn't really believed it until that instant. He hadn't wanted to believe it. An already hopelessly complicated, messy situation was rapidly getting worse.

He stood next to her. "Tell me what happened. Tell me the truth. Is Travis Rider dead?"

"No!"

"But he's hurt."

"Not very badly."

"Did you get him to a doctor?"

"Fred's a doctor, remember?"

"If he's all right, where is he? Why hasn't he shown up for this hearing? Why do you have his wallet in your car?"

Katie reached down and picked up the wallet, squeezing it in both hands. "You know, it's getting awfully late. We probably ought to round up Nathan and head back to the Andersons'. I know Mary's cooking dinner, and it would be really rude to be late."

He grasped her shoulders a second time and forced her to look at him. "You're not going to change the subject again. We need to talk about this. I'm on your side. I'm your husband. I don't care how this marriage started out. I love you. Whatever you've done, whatever we've done, we'll deal with it. We'll make it all right. But you've got to tell me the truth. Katie, where is Travis Rider?"

Chapter Nine

Katie's heart clenched into a hard little knot. It was over, she thought.

All of it. Her little charade, the outcome of the custody hearing... Everything depended on what Travis decided once he knew the truth. Wondering and worrying about this moment was over. Sleeping in the same bed as Travis was over. Kissing Travis, having Travis stand up for her and be on her side—everything was over.

For all the fear and panic she'd gone through anticipating this moment, now she felt only a cold, shocked numbness.

With stiff, reluctant fingers, she opened the wallet to his driver's license and handed it to him.

Travis stared down, then looked back up uncomprehendingly. "So what? Why shouldn't this guy's driver's license be in his wallet?"

Katie leaned over to look. The picture was terrible, a typical Texas driver's license issue, unrecognizable.

Reprieve! He didn't know it was his wallet. He still believed he was John Dunn. She could tell him they'd killed Travis Rider and—

She looked at his bewildered face and sighed. No, that wouldn't do. She'd pretty well played out this angle. It was time to confess. All she'd asked for was a few minutes to plead her case. Well, she'd had two days. *Time's up.*

"It's a lousy picture," she said, "but it's you."

Travis's brows drew together in confusion. "What? What are you saying?" He looked again at the license. "Travis Rider," he repeated slowly, lifting his startled gaze to hers.

His eyes seemed to focus inward then, and she knew even before he spoke that the event she'd been waiting for and dreading had arrived. He was remembering. John Dunn was leaving; Travis Rider was returning. Her husband was leaving; her enemy was returning.

She held her breath, afraid to disturb the process even while she feared the outcome.

He blinked and refocused on her. "You hit me," he said, his tone incredulous. "I was outside your house, and you hit me."

Katie laced her fingers and clasped her hands in front of her. She'd tried to prepare herself for this, but she hadn't done a very good job of it. She suspected the shock was almost as great to her as it was to Travis.

"Yes," she admitted, "I hit you. But I had a good reason. I thought you were a prowler. I thought you were going to shoot John."

"John?"

"The real John. Fred."

"The real John. Not me." He still sounded a little bewildered.

Small wonder, she supposed. This was his second personality switch in as many days. That was bound to be a little confusing.

"No," she said. "The real John's not you."

"I'm not John. I'm not a doctor. I'm a detective." He took a step backward, away from her, and sat down on the edge of the front seat of the car, his eyes never leaving hers. "We're not married." Did he sound just the tiniest bit disappointed? Probably not. There was certainly no reason he should. "I'm doing a job for your father. I heard you talking to that other guy—"

"John Dunn."

"Yeah. You were talking to him about pretending to be your husband. Only he had to work and couldn't make it." He was warming to the subject now, his expression becoming less perplexed with every word—and more angry. "I heard a noise behind me. I whirled around, and there you were, waving something in the air—"

"An iron skillet."

"An iron skillet?" He lifted a tentative hand to his head as if not quite believing. He flinched when he touched the sore spot. "You raised both hands over your head and deliberately hit me with an iron skillet." Uttering a string of curses, he stood abruptly. Involuntarily she moved back, away from his fury. "You could have killed me!"

Irritated with herself for her show of fear, she thrust out her chin defensively. "That was the general idea.

You had that microphone in your hand, and I thought it was a gun. I was protecting my friend."

He shook his head slowly. "If this wasn't happening to me, I wouldn't believe it was possible. Who were you protecting when you told me I was your husband?"

"I was protecting Nathan. I didn't expect it to go so far. I just wanted a few minutes to try to explain things so you wouldn't misinterpret what you'd heard while you were *snooping around my house.*" Might as well remind him that he'd been in the wrong first. He seemed to have forgotten that part.

"You wanted to make everybody believe you were married when you weren't. That sounds pretty clear-cut to me. How could I possibly misinterpret that?"

"Well, yes, I suppose that's basically true, but I had a good reason. I wanted you to hear that reason. John said you'd probably get your memory back in a few minutes, but I figured if we were on the way to Oklahoma, you'd be stuck with me long enough so that I could convince you not to testify against me."

"And what were you going to do if you couldn't convince me? Hit me with a car jack and leave my body in a ditch somewhere along Highway 75? Was that Plan B?"

"Of course not! I didn't have a Plan B. If Plan A failed, I wouldn't be any worse off than before. But I just knew if I could tell you the whole story, you'd understand. And you did. How many times have you said how much better parents we'd be—I'd be—than my father and mother? You've seen how much happier Nathan is with me. It would be a crime to sentence him to live with my parents."

In the bright, sunny day, Travis's face darkened with rage, his cold, furious glare an icy knife thrusting straight into her heart. She had obviously let herself become much too involved in her own fabrications. It felt as if someone she really loved was mad at her.

But she didn't love him. That was all a fantasy.

And the fantasy was over.

"You think what you did wasn't a crime?" he demanded. "Lying to me about my identity, letting me get into an argument with the man who hired me..." He stopped, his jaw clenching, his frown so intense his brows almost met over his nose. "Cuddling up to me in that bed last night," he went on, his voice now quiet but a hundred times more menacing. "Kissing me? Was that all part of Plan A?"

"*You* kissed *me,*" she accused. "At least, you started it," she amended in the interest of honesty. Why, all of a sudden, did she have a compulsion to tell the whole truth?

"You weren't exactly uncooperative."

Katie folded her arms over her chest and looked across the park to where Nathan and his friends were playing. Boy, when things started going downhill, they sure could accelerate rapidly. "Kissing you had nothing to do with my plan," she said, refusing to look him in the eye. "That was kind of an unexpected, uh, side effect, sort of. I told you, I only wanted a chance to convince you of what was right."

"What you did wasn't right."

She wasn't sure if he meant lying to him or kissing him. "Well, it wasn't exactly wrong. It seemed like a good idea at the time." That pretty well covered either one.

"Of course it was wrong!" He slapped the top of the car, the sound yanking her gaze back to him just in time to see him flinch and look at his hand.

Automatically she reached for his fingers. "Burn it on the hot metal?"

He yanked his hand away from her inspection, away from her. "It's fine."

"Serves you right for losing your temper that way," she snapped, lashing out to cover the inexplicable hurt his action brought her.

He ignored her remark. "Katie, how did you expect to get away with this? Even if you'd gotten custody, weren't you worried I'd come back and testify after I'd regained my memory? Or did you think maybe I'd never remember? Did you just plan to go on letting me believe I was your husband, the doctor? What would happen when I got back to Dallas and started to practice medicine? Don't you think somebody would have noticed?"

"Of course not," she said, meeting his sarcasm with her own. "I thought you could deliver babies and do Pap smears and join the country club and play golf and nobody would ever notice. I told you, Travis, I only planned to buy a few minutes. When you didn't get your memory back right away, I just kind of... improvised."

He loomed over her, his face grim, hands clenched at his sides. "That's exactly the kind of attitude Nathan doesn't need to be subjected to."

"What! You're not planning to take my father's side after everything you've learned, are you?"

"No, Katie. I'm not taking anybody's side. My only part—my only legitimate part—in this whole thing is to tell the judge what I know. I'm a detective. I leave the decisions to people better qualified than I am to make them."

Katie looked toward the baseball game again. Nathan crouched on third base, ready to steal home at the first opportunity. If she didn't do something fast, he might never make it to a real home. Her gaze darted around frantically.

Dash across the park, grab Nathan and make a run for it. Whack Travis over the head with—what? A soft-drink can? Somehow she doubted it had the capability of her iron skillet to trigger amnesia. She supposed she could always throw herself on Travis's mercy—assuming he had any—and beg.

None of those options seemed likely to produce the desired results.

"So what happens now?" she asked quietly.

He ran a hand through his hair, and her throat tightened painfully at the familiar gesture from this suddenly strange man. "I don't know," he said. "I've got to talk to your father."

"You can't do that!" she protested. "You know what he's like."

He looked at her then, his gaze harsh. This was not the same man who'd helped Nathan fly a kite or who'd kissed and held her so tenderly and called her *my Katie.*

"I know what his daughter is like, too. I know she hasn't been very honest."

"That's true but only if you assume that *honest* is a rigid, inflexible term. I've been totally honest in the spirit of things."

"The spirit of the law but not the letter."

"Yeah!" For an instant, hope flared.

"I think it's time we dealt with the truth according to the letter of the law."

She should have expected the man he'd turned back into would insist on a technicality. "And just what is that supposed to mean?"

For a split second, he looked a little unsure, as if he didn't quite know which way to go. But then his jaw thrust out squarely. "It means I need to talk to your father. He hired me to gather information for him."

The temptation crossed her mind to tell him to go for it. The six-mile walk to her father's house would be good for him. But she'd driven him where she wanted him to go. The only fair thing now would be to take him where he wanted to go.

"All right," she agreed from between clenched teeth. "Let me get Nathan." She took a step toward her nephew, then stopped and uttered a heartfelt oath, an oath lacking the expertise of Travis's earlier words but, she decided, making up for it in intensity. "What am I going to tell Nathan?" One look at Travis's stern face told her the answer. "I know. The truth. No matter how many innocent people it hurts."

She started across the park toward him. Suddenly her sore ankle was hurting again. And this time Travis wasn't going to rub it for her.

Travis watched Katie as she crossed the grass, her head high, slim shoulders erect, limping slightly. He watched her going unwillingly to tell an eight-year-old boy that the man he'd bonded with wasn't really his uncle, was, in fact, *the enemy*—at least in Katie's judgment.

Damn her! Because of her, he'd gotten to know the parties in this case, and now they weren't *parties* anymore; they were real people. Somehow this made him feel his job ought to be more than just delivering a report.

Well, it couldn't be. He was a detective, not a judge. He could only deliver the facts.

But his heart ached for the boy playing in the park. Nathan was an all right kid. He shouldn't have to endure first losing his parents and now facing all this.

"Katie!" He lunged after her, catching her only a few yards away. She hadn't been walking at her usual brisk pace.

"What?" she snapped, turning to him with a scowl.

"I'll go with you. We'll tell him together."

"I didn't need your help getting into this mess and I don't need it getting out." She whirled away.

He caught her arm. She looked at his fingers, then his face, her expression black. He jerked his hand away. "I'm not offering for your sake. I just think it might be easier for Nathan to hear this from both of us."

Her lips compressed tightly, and her eyes narrowed. He could read her struggle almost as clearly as if he were inside her mind.

"Damn it, Katie, don't be so pigheaded. You keep saying you want what's best for Nathan."

"How can you even presume to know what's best for him?" She spit the words at him.

"How can you?"

"I love him. That gives me some rights you don't have."

"I'll bet if you asked your father, he'd say he loves him, too."

"Yeah. He'd *say* it. As we've all seen over the past couple of days, just because you say something, that doesn't make it the truth."

Travis spread his hands in a gesture of surrender. "Fine. Have it your way. I'll find a phone somewhere and call a taxi while you tell Nathan the truth, then he and I will go to *my client's* house."

He turned his back to her and began walking. He'd try one of the houses across the street from the park. This was a small town; they'd probably still let a stranger use the phone. And then he was finished with Katie for good. He had no business spending even one more minute with her.

The fact that he didn't want to cut the connection so abruptly was just further evidence that he should. He'd settled much too deeply into the role of loving husband. He needed to put some distance between them and straighten out who he really was.

He'd taken only a few steps when her voice stopped him. "Not in this town you won't call a taxi. There isn't one. You're stuck with me for a chauffeur."

He hated the feeling of relief that washed over him. His contact with Katie wasn't broken yet.

Then his logical mind kicked in, pushing aside such irrational notions. He looked back at her. "I'll call your father to come pick us up."

"Don't do that. Please."

What was there about her that made him want to protect her from the world, from himself, to give her whatever she wanted, no matter how ridiculous it was?

"All right." As if from a distance, he heard himself say the words and noted the bittersweet anticipation of looking forward to this last trip, these last few minutes with Katie.

"Mary's making dinner for us, you know," she said. "You can at least let them see Nathan once more before you deliver him into the dragon's lair."

Travis rubbed the back of his neck. There was no point in arguing with her. "Okay. Let's get Nathan, and we'll go back to the Andersons'. We'll tell everybody together."

And then he was pretty sure he wouldn't be a welcome dinner guest. Even if he had an appetite, which he was certain he wouldn't. Maybe he could just wait outside on the curb...after he made sure Mary didn't own any iron skillets.

What the heck was the matter with him that he had to force back a smile at that thought? What Katie had done wasn't funny. He was very angry at her. If he saw the amusing side of her actions and was perversely pleased that he'd be with her for a while longer, that only meant that the bump on his head had messed up more than his memory.

It was fortunate, Katie thought, that on the way to Paul and Mary's, Nathan kept up a steady stream of chatter about his baseball game, necessitating only an occasional "Wow" or "Cool" from her. No way could she have carried on a coherent conversation.

Travis had nothing to say, but his unspoken accusations were so loud, she could almost hear them. She felt his angry gaze on her even though she kept her eyes fixed on the road ahead.

Already a sense of loss was eating a hole in her heart. Her "husband, John" was gone. Okay, so he'd never really existed. Nevertheless, irrationally, she missed him.

Her father had always told her that divine punishment was the consequence of telling lies. But he'd never mentioned the danger of getting caught up in those lies and beginning to believe them herself.

The ten-minute trip to the Andersons' house seemed to take an hour. Emotional turmoil definitely had an odd effect on the passage of time. Finally, she turned onto their street.

And saw a police car sitting in their driveway.

Panic flooded her veins, mingling with the tension, sadness and desperation already there and creating total chaos. She clutched the steering wheel so tightly, her fingers ached.

Had they come to get Nathan? Had her father worked some deal under the table? Or had they come to haul her off to jail for the murder of Travis Rider? If the latter, would he reveal his identity or just let them take her? Or would he tell them who he was and have her charged with assault and kidnapping and who knew what else? Impersonating a wife, forcing him to wear white boxer shorts?

"Why's the police here?" Nathan asked, his curious tone reflecting none of her panic.

"Maybe they're friends of your grandparents," Travis suggested.

"Yeah, my other grandpa—I mean, grandfather has a policeman friend."

That bit of information didn't help Katie's burgeoning nervous breakdown in the slightest. Her father had the judge and the police force in his corner. Not to mention her pseudo former husband.

Travis got out of the car and helped Nathan unload the kite and ice chest. Mary opened the front door of the house and stood waiting for them. Like an automaton, forcing one foot in front of the other, each step an effort, Katie followed Travis and Nathan up the walk.

"We have company," Mary said, a forced smile on her face, concern in her eyes.

Travis stepped back to allow Katie to enter first. Of all the times for him to be courteous...

Paul and two police officers, one of whom she recognized from high school, rose from the sofa. Each officer politely held his hat in one hand.

Katie had a sudden image of being executed by a firing squad, all of whom nodded politely before they fired.

"Hi, Katie," the younger officer greeted.

Katie's first attempt at speech came out a squeak. She cleared her throat and tried again. "Hi, Gerald."

"Haven't seen you since high school. Hear you left us and ran off to the big city. Uh, Katie, this is Melvin Morris. He's from Brockton. You remember how their football team was always our toughest opponent. Of course, Melvin graduated a few years before us, so you probably never saw him play."

Small towns, she thought. *I have to be properly introduced to somebody, along with information about his hometown, before he can handcuff me.*

She nodded toward the older, larger, hulking guy, obviously a former football player. "Hi, Melvin."

Melvin stuck his thumbs in his gun belt and swaggered. This didn't bode well at all. What was that old country song about being in jail and eating nothing but fried eggs, gravy and bologna? She could feel her cholesterol rising already.

"Mrs. Dunn, we need to ask you a few questions," Melvin said.

The room had become preternaturally silent. For all she knew, Travis, Nathan, Mary and Paul had disintegrated into thin air behind her. She felt as though she were standing alone in front of the two officers.

She took a deep breath. "Okay. Ask away."

Melvin handed over an even worse copy of Travis's driver's license picture. If Travis couldn't recognize himself from the original, these guys sure couldn't from this copy. Without his cooperation, she could never prove Travis was . . . Travis.

Unless she could give him a glass of wine, then save the glass for fingerprints. But right now he probably wouldn't accept a glass filled with diamonds from her.

"We just got this from Dallas, Texas," Melvin said. "Do you know this man?"

"Yes. I know him. It's Travis Rider."

Melvin and Gerald exchanged looks.

"When did you meet Mr. Rider?"

"Oh, a couple of days ago."

"Under what circumstances?"

"He was, uh, peeking in my window."

Another exchange of glances.

"Peeking in your window?"

"That's right. He's a private detective. He was detecting."

"What did you do when you caught him peeking in your window?"

She turned her head to check on Travis. He stood just behind her, arms folded across his chest, his lips compressed into a tight line. Surely he wasn't going to let this continue. Actually, from the expression on his face, he probably was. He appeared to find a grim amusement in the situation.

"Mrs. Dunn, Mr. Rider has disappeared. His last known appointment was at your house. His car was found abandoned three blocks from there. Do you want to tell us what you know, or do you want to go down to the station?''

To her surprise, she felt a familiar arm slip around her waist, caught the familiar masculine scent of Travis as he moved up to stand beside her.

''I'm Travis Rider, and, as you can see, I haven't disappeared. Haven't even lost any weight.''

With all the gasps in the room, the light-headed sensation that burst over Katie was probably from lack of oxygen.

She wanted to cry. It was so wonderful to have Travis on her side again, the way he had been every time she'd needed him for the past two days. So wonderful and so temporary. His touch was different this time. Impersonal, solid but not comforting. He was helping her, doing the right thing, but he wasn't really with her any longer.

''You're Travis Rider?'' Melvin looked from him to the picture and back again. Gerald came over and repeated the process.

Travis took his wallet from his back pocket and handed it over. ''Look at my P.I. license. The picture's a little better.''

The officers flipped through the cards, studied Travis again, then looked at each other and shrugged.

''If you're Travis Rider, why haven't you told anybody? Why'd you abandon your car? Why are you pretending to be somebody else?''

''I don't think I need to answer any of those questions. Leaving my car parked on the street for so long is the only crime that's been committed here. I can call myself by any name as long as I don't do it with criminal intent. If you'll return my wallet, I'll say good-night, gentlemen.'' Still holding her body against his,

Travis stepped aside, extending his hand for his wallet and allowing the officers access to the door.

Melvin clutched the wallet uncertainly. "Maybe you better come down to the station and let us make a more positive ID."

"Maybe you'd better come back with a warrant if you want me to do that or if you intend to confiscate my property."

Melvin glowered at him, but handed back the wallet and donned his cap. "Sorry to have bothered you, Mrs. Dunn. Uh, Mrs. Rider. Uh..."

"Bye, Katie," Gerald said.

Only when Mary had closed both the storm door and the wooden door behind the officers did anyone speak.

"What's going on?" she asked, her gaze flitting from Katie to Travis and back again.

"Katie has something to tell you," he said, then moved away from her. The separation might have been physical, a rending of one body from another, so raw did she feel where he no longer touched her.

Chapter Ten

When Katie pulled up in front of Ralph Logan's house, Travis knew he couldn't go inside. He'd gone through the agony of telling Nathan the truth and seen his young eyes fill with first sadness then hopelessness. Finally, he'd sat through the silent dinner at Paul and Mary's request, but nobody had eaten. Everyone had sat silently, pushing their food around on their plates. And all the time he'd been dreading this moment.

He knew what his duty was, but he also knew he couldn't be objective in that sterile building. He could easily lose his head and do or say something he shouldn't. Something crazy. As crazy as the way he'd defended Katie with the police.

He still didn't understand that. One minute he'd been enjoying watching her squirm, and the next he'd fallen back into the role of her fake husband, the role she'd trumped up. Habit, he supposed. Well, it was a habit he'd damn sure better break, and soon.

He turned to Nathan, who sat quietly in one corner of the back seat. "Listen, buddy, I have some things I need to do before I talk to your grandfather. Could you go on in by yourself, and I'll see you tomorrow?"

Nathan nodded and fumbled with the door handle without looking up.

"And, Nathan, let's not say anything to your grandfather about everything that's happened until I get a chance to call him, okay?"

Nathan nodded again.

Travis could feel the surprise emanating from Katie, but she said nothing, either, just climbed out of the car and walked up to the door with her nephew. As Travis watched, she leaned down and hugged the boy.

"I love you, sweet pea," she said. "Remember that. No matter what happens, I'll always be here for you."

The door opened, and again Travis's heart clenched as he watched Ralph Logan lead the boy inside and close the door behind them.

Katie stood on the porch for several seconds, then turned and walked slowly back to the car.

"What was that all about?" she asked as she settled behind the wheel.

"Would you mind taking me to the Sleepy Time Motel?"

She shrugged. "Sure. But I thought you were anxious to talk to your *client*."

"I have his phone number."

"I see."

As they made the seemingly long drive to the motel—surely not more than a ten-minute trip—Travis found himself marveling that he had felt so close to this woman, had never doubted that they were married, and now they were acting like strangers. People went from being strangers to being close, not the opposite.

Of course, the thing he really didn't understand was that somewhere deep in his gut, he still felt drawn to her. He was furious with her, of course. He wanted to scream and yell and storm and rage at her. But he was having a hard time shaking the feeling that she was his wife. As soon as he finished screaming and yelling, he wanted to kiss her and hold her and vent all that excess adrenaline by making wild love with her.

Hopefully, as his head healed, so would this bout of insanity. Maybe his doctor could give him some pills. Did they make anti-Katie pills?

"Well, here we are." She flinched at her own words, words she'd said when they'd driven up the first time—when he'd been eager with the anticipation of spending the night with his "wife." "Guess I've said that before," she muttered nervously.

"Yes, you have," he replied brusquely. At least, that was how he hoped his reply sounded. Brusque, not confused, the way he felt.

He reached for the handle of the door. All he had to do was open it and get out, and Katie would be gone from his life forever. Other than at the hearing, he'd never again have to see this woman who'd lied to him. Actually, *lied* didn't even begin to describe what she'd done to him.

"Nathan sure didn't want to go in there tonight," she said.

He had to give her credit. She never stopped trying, never accepted defeat.

"I know. Katie, it may not be the best home in the world, but it's probably not the worst, either."

Katie's left eyebrow quirked upward. "You certainly have changed your tune. If I may be permitted to refresh your flagging memory, not long ago you were all in favor of my having custody of Nathan."

"Not long ago I didn't have all the facts."

"You most certainly did," she protested. "I told you everything about Nathan and about my father and about me. Except, of course, that I'm going to be a single mother. But that's inconsequential."

"Yes," he agreed, "it is. The tiny little detail that I was missing was my identity. I'm not your husband. I'm not Nathan's uncle. I don't have the right to fight for him. The only right I have is to tell the court what I know about this case."

"And doom Nathan just because my methods of trying to make things right can sometimes be a little unorthodox."

That was, he thought, a major understatement.

"Don't be melodramatic. Nathan isn't going to be doomed, not even if your father gets custody. You survived living with the man. I'll tell you what, Katie, at Nathan's age, I'd have given anything for a home to come to day after day, year after year. I would have loved to be able to make friends that I could meet at the park and play ball with. I never knew from one day to the next what town we'd be in, where we'd be living, whether we'd be eating steak in a posh restaurant or peanut butter sandwiches while dodging the landlord. I never knew who my next stepfather would be. There's something to be said for stability, for a predictable world to hang on to."

"I would never do that to Nathan! I told you!"

"Every move we made, my mother swore it would be the last, we'd settle down and make a home. Then she'd meet a new guy or hear about a new job or—hell, one time she didn't want to defrost the refrigerator, so we moved to another apartment with a frost-free."

Katie didn't answer, just sat quietly in the darkness, her eyes luminous.

"You've done that, haven't you?" he accused, taking her silence for guilt. After all, she was guilty of so much.

"Certainly not! I've never even used the freezer for anything except ice cubes, and not many of them. It's too hard to poke an ice cube down the little hole in the cola can."

He stared at her for a second, then, against his will, he burst into laughter. She joined him, and it was a relief from the terrible tension, but it wasn't the free and easy laughter they'd shared when they'd been living her lie. Soon it trickled into a strained silence.

"I only moved from one thing to another when I got bored," she said defensively. "When I wanted to try something new."

"And you think you won't get bored taking care of a growing boy, going to PTA meetings and baseball games, cooking meat loaf, using the freezer for something besides ice cubes?"

"No," she said quietly. "I love Nathan. I could never get bored with him."

My mother said she loved me, too, he wanted to shout. *But it wasn't enough for her.* Even knowing that, he had to fight to keep from succumbing to the sincerity in her eyes.

He yanked on the door handle and climbed out of the car. He had to get clear of Katie and back to reality. He closed the door, then leaned down to look in the window.

"Uh, thanks for the ride over." Now what did he say? *See you in court?*

"You're welcome." She hesitated. "Goodbye." She put the car in gear and pulled away. A little too fast, he thought, but that was Katie.

The room he checked into wasn't the same one they'd shared, but it looked identical. Well, almost. Unlike the other, it seemed to have a dingy, sad air about it.

He lay on top of the bedspread for a long time, telling himself over and over how lucky he was that his marriage to Katie hadn't been real. Undoubtedly because his mind was still foggy from his injury, it kept rebelling against him.

Katie had done a damn good job of convincing him they were married. By making him believe he was her husband, she'd allowed him to experience emotions he wouldn't normally have felt. Bogus emotions, but emotions he was having a hard time shaking.

In self-defense, he reviewed the evening he'd stood outside her window and how certain he'd been of her inadequacies. Her recent actions, even more than her past, proved she was, well, *flaky.* He definitely didn't need any more of that.

Finally, he worked himself up to the point where he was able to call Ralph Logan.

Katie returned to Paul and Mary's to find them both sitting in the living room. The television was dark and silent. Just the way she felt.

She flopped onto the sofa next to Mary and picked up a magazine, though she certainly had no intention of reading. "Guess I blew it, huh?"

Mary gave her a quick hug. "Don't be too hard on yourself. You did what you thought was best at the time. I'm afraid the cards have been stacked against us—against Nathan—from the beginning."

"Damn it, that's not fair! There must be something we can do!"

Paul shook his head slowly. "Sometimes, Katie, there isn't anything that can be done. I know that's hard for you to accept. You've always been such a *doer.* But I'm afraid it's up to the judge now."

"And Travis."

"And Travis," Paul admitted. "What he says will probably have an influence on the judge."

With nervous fingers, Katie drummed the padded arm of the sofa and let out a long sigh. "Yeah, I'd say the odds are pretty good on that. I'm sorry. This is all my fault."

"Of course it's not all your fault," Mary reassured her. "You thought you were doing the right thing. I might have tried it, too, if I'd had the imagination to think of it. I do have one question, though. Why did you think it was necessary to pretend to have a husband in the first place?"

"Because I asked the social worker what else I could do to better my odds. And she said the only thing I didn't have was a husband, so I thought I'd get one. With my past and the fact that my father is such a pillar of the community, I figured I needed every advantage possible."

"Well, yes, your father is a problem. But what's wrong with your past? Is there something we don't know?"

Katie grinned wryly. "You mean something like assault? No, that's a new item I've added to my repertoire just recently."

"Then what?"

"You know. The way I kind of flit from one thing to another. I haven't exactly had what you might call a *stable* life-style. Fun, but not very stable."

"According to who?" Paul asked. "Ralph Logan? You need to stop even considering his opinion."

"Katie," Mary said, "we know everything about you. We're very conservative people, and we think you'd make a wonderful mother for Nathan."

Katie's eyes misted. She stood and went to hug first Mary then Paul. "Thank you both," she said, "for believing in me. We three may be the only people in the world who do."

"Nathan does," Mary reminded her. "And Becky and Darryl. And tomorrow we'll convince the judge."

"Right."

Paul and Mary went on to bed, and Katie trudged up the stairs to sleep in Darryl's old room. Alone. At least she didn't have to worry about sleeping with Travis tonight.

Somehow, that thought wasn't as comforting as it should have been. Suddenly—well, not really so suddenly, she realized something. Starting from the time she'd let Travis out of the car at the Sleepy Time Motel, she'd felt alone, deserted.

She shook her head and smiled at her own silliness.

When you tell a lie, you really go all the way, don't you? she berated herself. *Get all involved in your own make-believe story.*

Well, Travis *wasn't* her husband, so he couldn't have deserted her. She'd always been entirely on her own, which was the way she wanted it.

She stepped onto the landing. The door to Darryl's room loomed just as large as it had the night before. All she'd accomplished was to exchange one set of worries for another.

She entered the room and closed the door behind her, then sat down on the bed. After two sleepless nights, she should be able to zonk out, but she doubted that was going to happen. Between fretting over Nathan's fate and dealing with her unnatural, insane feelings about Travis, she should be totally familiar with every crack in the ceiling by morning.

Ironically, after all these years of working so hard to be in control of her own life, she seemed to be right back in the position she'd tried so hard to escape. If she were to believe the Andersons and Travis, she was still allowing her father to control her life, even if indirectly.

She wasn't too sure she accepted that, but she couldn't deny that Travis was in control of Nathan's fate and, consequently, hers. She'd always known she would never have a serious relationship, certainly not one that involved marriage, because she would never again allow someone to control her. And now someone had that control—and he wasn't even her real husband.

Her earlier assumption that Becky's angel was watching over this whole business was obviously in error. An angel would never be this sadistic.

She changed into her big nightshirt, the one she'd felt so sexy wearing in Travis's presence last night. Tonight, like the rest of her life, it just felt big and empty.

She lay down on the bed and lifted her hand to turn out the light. The cheap wedding band mocked her, its finish already tarnished. She pulled it from her finger and set it on the nightstand, then switched off the lamp.

Damn! If this was what it was like to go through an imaginary marriage and divorce, she sure never wanted to have a real one!

Katie shifted on the hard courtroom bench, though no amount of shifting was going to make it comfortable—neither for her almost-numb rear nor for her totally jangled nerves.

It was nearly three o'clock, and the hearing had been going on since nine that morning. With the exception of an hour's break for lunch, she'd been sitting there beside Brad Fletcher, working her way well into the middle of that nervous breakdown.

The court's advocate had presented the findings of the state agency. Katie, her father, Mary, Paul, half a dozen people had testified on her father's behalf, and even Nathan had given their testimony.

Everyone except Travis.

So far, she thought, it looked good for her. Even though Nathan had been kept away from the courtroom until his turn to testify, he had, in his child-wise way, verified everything she, Paul and Mary had said. He had politely but adamantly asked to be permitted to live with his Aunt Katie.

Yesterday the judge had shown himself to be impartial at least to a small degree. If only Travis had developed a conscience during the night, or another case of amnesia, Nathan might have a chance.

"Your Honor," Winters said, and the smirk in his voice squashed her embryonic hope, "we'd like to call our last witness, Travis Rider, my client's private detective."

She turned toward the back of the courtroom and saw him stride through the doorway in the leather jacket and jeans he'd worn that first night. He looked so familiar, so dependable, so dear.

Dependable? Dear? Those were certainly odd terms to describe the instrument of her destruction.

Chapter Eleven

Travis made his way down the aisle of the courtroom, purposely averting his gaze from the bench where he knew Katie would be seated.

He'd been sequestered in a room down the hall for most of the day. The practice was, he knew, to avoid the possibility that a witness might be swayed by the testimony of other witnesses. That wasn't even a possibility for him, but he hadn't minded not being forced to sit for hours in the same courtroom with Katie. The same courtroom where he'd sat beside her, where he'd believed himself to be her husband. He was still having a difficult time getting the fog out of his head on that subject, and the farther he was away from her, the easier it would be.

Besides, he didn't want to see the look of betrayal he knew would be blatantly evident on her face. And he hated himself for feeling that way because he was the one who'd been betrayed.

When the bailiff had come to get him to present his testimony, he'd passed Nathan being taken somewhere by another officer of the court. Nathan had smiled tentatively and greeted him with a "Hi, Uncle—" then stopped in midsentence and quickly looked away.

As Travis took the witness stand and swore to tell the truth, he wasn't even sure he knew the truth anymore. It had seemed so simple the night he'd been eavesdropping outside Katie's window. But Katie had managed to stand The Truth on its ear.

He answered Winters's questions as honestly and tactfully as he could, giving his credentials and the details of his investigation. To his surprise, he found himself trying to excuse Katie's actions.

"She thought I was a prowler with a gun, so she hit me with an iron skillet."

"She wanted a chance to talk to me, so she told me we were married."

Only once did he look in Katie's direction. When asked to identify the woman he'd been investigating, he focused on the top of her shimmering blond hair, avoiding her eyes.

But as much as his gazc refused to settle on Katie, just as strongly was it drawn to Ralph Logan. The man looked stern, cold and unapproachable. If he'd met him in person rather than over the telephone, he doubted that he'd have taken this job.

The first time he'd seen Logan, the night the man had appeared as a silhouette in the doorway, come to take an unwilling Nathan, he'd disliked him. In fact, that meeting had almost called up a memory. For just a second, he'd thought Logan was someone else, someone trying to draw him inside.

He tried to concentrate on that moment, to recall what he hadn't been able to pin down at the time.

Like a ghost appearing then disappearing, the face of Travis's father flashed across Logan's.

Amazing! He'd resented his mother's life-style for so long, he'd forgotten that he'd begged to go with her when his parents had divorced. She hadn't really wanted to take him, had tried to force him to stay with his father. But he'd known, even at the age of six, that his stern father would suffocate him. Later, his father's home and stability had seemed desirable. However, the man had never forgiven his son's desertion, so he'd never been allowed to return, even for a visit.

"Mr. Rider? I said, you may step down now."

"What? Oh." He stood and started to leave the witness stand, then stopped. "Your Honor, may I be permitted to address the court concerning the matter before it?"

"Certainly, Mr. Rider. Remember, you're still under oath."

Travis sat down again. Winters regarded him suspiciously. Travis returned his attention to the judge.

"I've had a chance most people in my profession never get. I've been able to study my subject up close. Real close. Closer than the court's advocate, closer than the Andersons. I've seen Katie Logan interact with Nathan—"

"Objection!" Winters exclaimed. "Your Honor, Mr. Rider is a private detective, not a social worker. He's given us the facts he uncovered. That's all he's qualified to do in this court."

Judge Grimes hesitated, his forehead wrinkled. Travis felt—hoped—that the man wanted to hear what he had to say.

"I'm not testifying as a detective now," Travis said quickly. "I'm testifying as a character witness. I'm as qualified for that as anyone else."

"I object!"

"The court notes your objection, Mr. Winters. Now the court will decide on the matter, if that's acceptable to you."

"Yes, Your Honor," Winters mumbled.

"We've heard testimony from several people in the capacity of character witnesses, people who know the parties to varying degrees. I see no reason why Mr. Rider's experience should be excluded. I'll allow you to testify in that capacity, Mr. Rider."

Travis again turned his attention to the judge. He couldn't look at Logan or at Katie. He had to keep this as impersonal as possible. And that wasn't going to be easy.

"Since I've been out of the courtroom all day, I have no idea what was said earlier. But the questions you've asked me have concerned Katie Logan's education, her friends, her job, her house, her potential for stability. Having lived as Katie's husband for two days, I'll be the last person to deny that she's somewhat impulsive and, uh, prone to handle situations in a unique manner." Damn! Had he caught Katie's talent for understatement?

"I can't honestly say whether I believe Katie can settle down the way she says she can and be a suitable mother."

He could feel her gaze on him, burning a hole through him. He hesitated, resisting the urge to look at her, to try to discern her unpredictable thoughts. Surely she wouldn't come after him with a skillet in the courtroom.

On the other hand, nothing was *sure* with Katie.

"Maybe it isn't pleasant for a little kid to be yanked around the countryside, thrown into school with a bunch of strangers, then yanked out just as he starts to make friends. But let me tell you what's worse than that. Not being loved. Maybe Katie hasn't got such a hot track record as far as stability, but she's got plenty of love.

"How do you even begin to measure the love of someone who's willing to tell a stranger he's her husband, to drive through the night with that stranger, stay in a motel room with him, keep up the pretense even when she could be charged with murdering that stranger? Katie can give Nathan all the love he'll ever need. More than enough to make up for any, shall we say, slightly unconventional methods of dealing with life."

As he left the witness stand, Travis avoided looking at Katie for a different reason than when he'd come in. He could too easily imagine her beautiful, shining eyes full of gratitude. He could too easily imagine being sucked into those eyes, into the fantasy of love she'd woven around the two of them for that brief, insane trip into illusion—a trip from which he'd emerged trailing wispy fragments.

That evening when the knock came on his motel room door, Travis caught himself heaving a sigh of relief. He'd known it could never be that simple where Katie was involved; he'd been waiting for that second shoe to drop ever since he left the courtroom.

He opened the door, knowing she'd be standing there, and she was—wearing cutoffs and a hot pink

T-shirt, looking innocent and uncomplicated. What a disguise.

"Hi," she said, her smile tentative as she shifted from one foot to the other. "I wanted to thank you for what you did."

"You don't need to thank me. I told the truth. That's all."

"Well, yeah, but your concept of the truth kind of underwent a major transformation overnight."

Now it was his turn to shift uncomfortably. "Okay, so maybe the truth isn't always an absolute." He stepped aside. This wasn't going to be a conversation that could be carried on while she stood outside. "Come in," he invited, and was dismayed when a thrill shot through him at the idea of once again being in a motel room with Katie.

It was all a lie, he reminded himself. *She's not your wife. You're not in love with her. Get a grip, man!*

"Have a seat." His words came out more harshly than he'd intended—harsh with himself, not her, but he didn't think it would be a good idea to point that out.

She stood for a moment looking around the room, and he realized there was no chair. Before he could invite her to sit on the bed, she sank gracefully to the floor, her sleek, tanned legs crossed in front of her.

"I wanted to apologize for hitting you," she said. "Although I had plenty of reason to do it, what with your sneaking around my house that way. But I shouldn't have lied to you. I apologize for that. I can only say that it seemed like a good idea at the time."

He felt awkward standing over her, so he sat beside her, a careful two feet away. "Have you ever thought that maybe you're a little too impulsive sometimes?"

She exhaled a long breath. "Yeah, maybe. If I've blown the deal with Nathan, I'll never forgive myself."

She looked so forlorn. He wanted to take her in his arms and comfort her, assure her everything would be all right. But that scenario was a really bad idea for two reasons. For one, in spite of his plea to the court in her favor, he had no idea how the judge was going to rule.

However, the main reason he sat on his hands and didn't budge from his spot of brown shag carpet was that he didn't dare take her into his arms. There was nothing wrong with his memory now, and the scene from their first night together in a bed just like the one two feet away was all too vivid. Getting his head to realize that they weren't in love was hard enough, but his hormones absolutely refused to listen to reason.

When he didn't say anything, she stood abruptly. "Well," she said, too brightly, "I'd better go. I just wanted to tell you that I really am sorry about deceiving you and—" she waved her hands distractedly "—everything that happened because of it."

Everything that happened because of it. Whew. That covered a lot of territory.

He stood. "Apology accepted." Two inane words. That's all he could say when a million more were trying to push their way out, most of them having to do with that *everything that happened because of it.* Better not even to think about them, much less say them aloud and make things more complicated than they already were.

She smiled tightly and lifted her shoulders in a shrug. "Okay. Good. Well. Guess I better be going. I already said that, didn't I?"

She darted to the door. He followed and stood in the open doorway watching her cross the cracked concrete parking lot. It wasn't as if she was leaving him; he couldn't lose something he'd never had. Once he went back to work, back to his life, this would all fall into its rightful place. It was kind of like being in a play. An actor worked so hard to become the character he was portraying that sometimes it was hard to leave the role behind when the play was over.

She reached her car, stopped and turned around, then ran over to him and threw her arms around him. Her body was warm and familiar and real... and before he had time to drink in the sensation, she dashed away.

Impulsive. Completely impulsive. Not good. This whole crazy situation came from her impulsiveness, and that last action hadn't helped anything.

He turned back into the room, closing the door behind him. *A role in a play.* He repeated the words over and over, waiting for his heart to stop pounding, for his stupid hormones to subside.

The next morning as she, Mary and Paul entered the courtroom, Katie scanned the empty rows. Her parents hadn't arrived yet, and, of course, Travis wasn't there. Not that there was any reason he should be. He'd done his thing yesterday. He had no further interest in the case.

The courtroom felt cold and hollow as she walked down the aisle. Even though she knew Mary and Paul were right behind her, she felt alone and isolated as she took her seat in her usual spot on the left front bench. The wood seemed even harder than yesterday. Not surprising, she supposed, since today was the day Judge Grimes would announce his decision.

She heard the door open, and whirled around, for a split second expecting to see Travis.

Her parents stepped through the door with Nathan tucked safely between them and their lawyer. They needn't have worried. She wouldn't have tried to see him. She couldn't bear to look into his eyes for fear that he had realized she might have let him down, that the judge might order him to stay with her parents.

Brad Fletcher followed her parents in—suspiciously close, she thought. Travis had probably been right about his being in her father's employ. Fletcher sat beside her and, fortunately, had the good sense to say nothing. One falsely kind word from him, and she didn't think she'd have been able to restrain herself from punching him in his prissy little mouth. Where was a good iron skillet when you needed one?

The judge entered the courtroom looking grim and solemn. Katie had to remind herself that he always looked that way.

From the row behind, Mary patted her shoulder. She and Paul had been wholeheartedly kind and supportive. But Katie knew they were just as upset as she, just as worried about the outcome.

"After giving due consideration to all the facts of this case, I have reached a decision. You, Ralph Logan, can offer a home where you've lived for thirty years, a stable environment, a place in the community, a two-parent home, a lot of things that are important to the welfare of the minor child."

Katie's knotted, tangled heart sank to the pit of her stomach.

"You, Miss Logan, are young, and that's in your favor. You would be more in touch with the needs of the minor child. On the other hand, you offer a home where you've lived for two months, a possibly unstable environment, a single-parent home in a large city."

He paused, and Katie clenched her hands, digging her nails into her palms to keep from crying out in protest at the unfairness. This couldn't be happening. How could she ever face Nathan again? How could she ever face herself again?

"I was very impressed with the fact that Mr. Rider, your father's witness, a man to whom you dealt bodily harm and whom you deceived, was willing to put in a good word for you. After that feat, I have to believe you'll succeed at anything you attempt."

He leveled his gaze first on Katie, then her father. "After due consideration of all the evidence, I have determined that the more desirable environment for the minor child would be the one provided by Miss Logan. I hereby award primary custody of Nathan Anderson to Katherine Logan, beginning now."

He scowled in Ralph Logan's direction as though anticipating a problem. "I also order liberal visitation for both sets of grandparents. I trust you'll be able to work that out between your attorneys. If not, I will be happy to intervene." He banged his gavel. "Case closed."

Katie catapulted from her seat. They'd won! The impossible had happened! All was right with the world!

She whirled around, for a fraction of a second expecting to throw herself into Travis's arms to celebrate their victory... but of course he wasn't there. Force of habit. That's all it was.

She turned to hug Paul and Mary, then charged across the courtroom to Nathan.

The boy still sat quietly, but when he saw her, he jumped up, cast a fearful look at his grandfather and ran to meet her. "I get to go home with you?" he asked, embracing her fiercely.

"You sure do, kiddo. You sure do."

Over Nathan's head, she dared to look at her father, then her mother. As expected, they sat stoically, no rebellious expressions revealing what they did or didn't feel.

"We'll have his clothes packed and ready by noon if you'd like to come by and pick them up," her father said.

"That'll be fine. I'm sure he'll want the chance to say goodbye to you. Though, of course, he'll be coming back to visit often. The judge said *liberal visitation.*" Good grief. Was she really trying to console her father? He was the last person in the world to need consolation. But it made her feel good—sort of clean inside—to offer it, and for the first time, she felt really free of him.

As she started out with Nathan, she saw Travis standing at the back of the room. He smiled and lifted his right thumb in a gesture of success. Then he turned and walked away, disappearing through the big door.

She knew she was being irrational, but suddenly she no longer felt that everything was right with the world.

"Are we ever going to see Uncle John—I mean Travis again?" Nathan asked.

Katie swallowed hard and forced herself to speak. "No, sweetheart, we're not. I'm sorry that I brought him into your life when I knew he couldn't stay. I just never thought you'd like him so much."

This would be harder for Nathan than for her, she told herself. Nathan had formed a genuine bond with Travis. The two had been buddies for real.

Right now her heart was aching for the husband she seemed to have lost. But that was an ersatz emotion. She'd never had a husband. She'd lied to everyone, including herself. And as soon as everything settled down to normal again, she'd be able to comprehend that, to get it through her stressed-out head...and heart.

She'd forget Travis Rider completely. She wouldn't remember the way he'd stood beside her through every problem, even when he was angry with her. She'd be unable to recall the width and solidity of his chest, the way his body felt against hers, the way his mouth felt on hers....

Okay, so she hadn't forgotten yet. When she got back home—when she and Nathan got back home—then she'd stop missing him, stop feeling as though she'd just lost a piece of herself.

Chapter Twelve

Travis came out of his mental fog just as he steered his car around a corner.

He ground out a swear word. He'd done it again, somehow made his way to Katie's street.

In the two months since the custody hearing in Oklahoma, his car had seemed to develop a magnetic pull to her house every time he got anywhere near her neighborhood. He'd driven past half a dozen times. He'd never stopped, of course. There was no reason to. His car's attraction to her house made as much sense as his attraction to her.

Against his will, he searched the yard and the porch for a glimpse of Katie. After all this time, after getting back to his real life, he still couldn't kick that insane feeling that they were in love. Maybe if he saw her again, he'd be able to get a grip on reality. That was probably why he kept returning to her house, he reasoned. He was hoping for a glimpse of the real woman to displace the fantasy woman, his fantasy wife.

But, as usual, he saw no sign of her.

He passed the house, casting one last glimpse in the rearview mirror.

Somebody was climbing onto the back side of the garage roof!

He stopped the car and twisted around in the seat for a better look. No, the figure was too small to be Katie, and the sun didn't bounce off shiny blond hair. It must be Nathan. What on earth was the boy doing up there? Where was Katie?

Then Nathan stood and spread his arms to reveal a web of some sort attached to his arms and his sides. As Travis watched in horror and astonishment, Nathan began to flap his arms, the web billowing—and jumped off the back of the garage!

Travis slammed the car into reverse, stopped in front of Katie's house and charged around to the rear, his heart racing. What if Nathan was hurt? Where the devil was Katie? Why hadn't she been watching him? He knew she was flaky, but he'd thought she'd take good care of Nathan. Damn!

"Travis!"

He came to a skidding halt just as he rounded the back corner of the garage. Standing beside a trampoline where Nathan bounced unharmed, Katie in a red tank top and cutoffs, eyes wide with surprise, looked every bit as tempting as the fantasy woman he remembered. She was real, flesh and blood, and seeing her did nothing to dispel his delusions. Quite the contrary. He wanted to close the distance between them, hold her in his arms and never let her get away again. Coming here had been a mistake—big-time.

"Uncle John! I mean Travis!" Nathan exclaimed, and vaulted off the trampoline to run over and hug him.

Travis tried to return the hug, but the plastic, which he now noticed had feathers glued on here and there, got in the way.

"I'm learning to fly," Nathan said, stepping back and flapping what Travis suddenly realized must be homemade wings.

Travis looked from the boy to the garage roof and the trampoline beneath. "Fly? You can't—"

"Nathan has, up to this point, failed to master flight," Katie said firmly, hands on her hips, daring him to deny the possibility of future success.

"But I dreamed about it, and Aunt Katie said if you can dream it, you can do it." Nathan beamed, obviously unperturbed by his inability to conquer flight—up to this point.

What the heck. Nobody thought Wilbur and Orville Wright could fly, either. At least Katie had seen to it that he didn't hurt himself while he tried.

And he couldn't deny that sometimes Katie's words were like magic. Reality had a way of conforming to her instead of the other way around. Like when she whacked him over the head and told him he was her husband. From that time onward, he'd been her husband in spite of something as inconsequential as reality.

"I didn't expect to see you here," Katie said. That made them even. He sure hadn't expected to be there. "Would you, uh, like to come in?" She looked as confused as he felt.

No, he said. At least that's what he planned to say, but somehow the word that came out of his mouth sounded more like "Yes."

It must have been yes since Katie, looking even more confused and something else he couldn't quite get a handle on—happy? excited?—turned and started for the door.

Well, he couldn't refuse now. He'd have to go with her. He had a sinking yet oddly buoyant feeling as though he were preparing to climb out of an airplane at ten thousand feet and wasn't positive his parachute would open.

Whatever, it was bound to be one hell of a ride.

Katie led Travis through the back door of her house. For just an instant when she'd looked up to see him charging toward her, she'd thought she was hallucinating. So often over the past two months, she'd turned to say something to him—and been momentarily startled to find he wasn't really at her side.

Everywhere she went, everything she did, she had to constantly fight the absurd notion that Travis was there beside her. She understood what was happening, of course. He'd been there during a very traumatic situation, and his presence had become imprinted. That explained everything. Even the way she reached for him every morning when she first woke up.

That explained it, but it didn't make the irritating experience any easier to endure. Her head knew what was going on, but her absurd heart actually thought she missed him, had actually gone wild with excitement when she looked up and saw him.

"Want to see my fossils?" Nathan asked as they passed the kitchen table where his microscope sat.

"We've been finding fossils in the backyard. Did you know this was all covered by the ocean a long time ago? Come on, I'll show you. You can see little bitty shells in the limestone that look just like the big ones we found on the beach at Padre Island."

Travis obligingly paused and looked through the microscope. "Hey! That's pretty cool, buddy."

"I'm going to be a geologist. We went to Carlsbad Caverns and saw the stalactites and stalagmites. You know how to remember which is which? Stalactites come down from the ceiling, and they have to hang on tight."

Travis nodded, smiling at the boy in a way that made Katie's insides go all soft and mushy. His affection for Nathan was genuine.

His affection for her, and hers for him, had, of course, been pretend. She only wished she could stop pretending. His unexpected arrival here probably wasn't going to help matters any.

"Want to see some more fossils?"

"Nathan, why don't you go outside and play for a while?" Katie suggested.

Nathan sighed. "I'll be glad when I'm grown so I won't have to leave the room while grown-ups talk about the interesting stuff. Can I have a cola?"

"That's blackmail, young man," Katie teased, pointing an accusing finger at him.

"Yeah, I know. Can I have one?"

"Well, as long as you understand the term, I guess so."

"Thanks!" He yanked open the refrigerator, grabbed a can and dashed out the back door, wings billowing.

Katie glanced at Travis and shrugged. "My nephew, the future criminal. At least he'll have a marketable skill." She leaned out the door. "Don't fly anymore until I get there! I want to be sure and be watching the first time you take off and soar!"

"Okay!"

She turned back to Travis, suddenly feeling uncomfortable now that they were alone. The past two months she'd kept unaccountably sensing his presence, and now that he was actually here beside her, they might have been strangers. Which, of course, they were.

"Well, come on in and have a seat." She gestured toward the living room. *And tell me why you're here.*

"Thanks." He strode over to the sofa, then hesitated.

Good grief. Hadn't the man ever seen a few toys before? She went past him to move Nathan's helmet, elbow pads and knee pads from the sofa onto the floor beside his in-line skates.

He sat down, then looked up at her with a wry smile. "I like entering your house a lot better this way than being dragged in unconscious."

She gave a short, nervous laugh. He was joking. She could tell that from the smile. She hoped he was joking. Had he come by because he was still angry about that little incident? Somehow, in all her imaginary conversations and meetings with Travis, that issue hadn't arisen.

She crossed the room and picked up Nathan's soccer ball from the armchair. Perching gingerly, she stayed as close to the edge as possible, not making a total commitment to sitting until she heard what he had to say, why he'd suddenly appeared in her yard.

"So, how've you been, Katie?"

"Good. And you?" She continued to hold the ball, her fingers tracing nervous circles on its cool, rubbery surface.

"Good."

Well, they were really making progress now.

"Would you—" she began at the same time as he started to speak.

"I'm sorry," he said. "Go ahead."

"Would you like a cold drink?" she asked.

"No, thanks."

"Okay, now you go ahead," she said, determined to make him say whatever it was he had to say. After all these weeks of trying to convince herself she and Travis had no real connection, was he about to do the job thoroughly and painfully for her?

"I thought you'd be interested to know that you got a lot of things right," he said, shifting his position. He didn't have a soccer ball to stroke. "I just thought you'd want to know that. Like when you told me I used to be a policeman. That was true. I did. That's where I got the scar on my stomach."

"A lucky guess. I really had no idea. But obviously you didn't leave the force to become a doctor and heal the people you used to shoot. I didn't get that part right."

"No. I left because I couldn't stand the bureaucracy. I never shot anybody."

"Fifty percent accuracy. I'll never make it as a psychic with those kinds of stats."

He nodded, leaned forward, laced his fingers, unlaced them, leaned back, and finally she couldn't stand it any longer. "What are you doing here? Not that I'm not happy to see you, but—"

He stood and shook his head. "I'll be damned if I know what I'm doing here." He paced across the room and looked out the window. "Those two days when I thought we were married, I really believed you, Katie. I believed you with all my heart. I believed we were married, and I believed I loved you. Even when I found out the truth, I couldn't kick the habit of believing."

"That's amazing!" She rose impulsively, laid down the soccer ball and went to stand beside him. "Me, too! It's like I accepted my own lies!"

He turned to look at her, his gaze appealing and baffled, his entire body, even his face, tense. "I kept telling myself that as soon as we were apart and I wasn't seeing you and being reminded of you all the time, as soon as my head healed, so would this crazy delusion."

"Exactly! That's exactly what I thought! Not that I had a head wound to heal, but other than that it's been the same for me."

He visibly relaxed. "No kidding? You, too? And this feeling just won't go away. I keep expecting to find you beside me. I start to tell you something, but you're not there. I went to a movie, and when they had a funny part, I turned to the empty seat beside me to share the laugh with you."

"Yes," she agreed excitedly. "That's just how it's been with me! Nathan and I went to Carlsbad Caverns, and at the frozen waterfall, I turned to this man beside me and took his arm, thinking it was you! He was real nice about it, but his wife glared at me. Oh, man, it's such a relief to be able to talk to somebody about this! I thought I was going nuts!"

A small smile tilted the corners of his mouth. "It does feel good to finally talk about it." His voice, his gaze, were so warm and personal, she wanted to reach out to him, touch him, wrap her arms around him....

Good grief. There she went again. What was it about this man? The *game* had been over for two months. When was she going to quit playing?

She turned away from him to stare unseeingly out the window. "I read somewhere that one lie would make a thousand ripples. I just never knew they meant like this."

His hand touched the back of her neck, lifting her hair. "You're letting your hair grow," he said, his breath warm on her neck.

She shrugged. "I always wanted to have long hair, and it suddenly seemed dumb to deprive myself of something I wanted just because my father had wanted the same thing. I guess you were right about my letting him still control my life. So we're even. I was right about your scar, and you were right about my father." She didn't know what that had to do with anything, but she felt a need to keep talking.

"I hope that doesn't mean you're planning to change completely," he said. "What you told Nathan about flying was kind of neat even if it was a little unconventional."

She spun around to face him, to challenge him. "I thought you didn't approve of unconventional."

"I never said that."

"Sure you did. Remember? Moving because the refrigerator needed defrosting?"

"I didn't know you very well then. We'd only been married two days." His eyes widened in horror and he took a step backward, then ran a hand distractedly through his hair. "What am I saying? I meant I didn't understand the situation. You love Nathan. That's what was missing from my relationship with my mother—genuine caring. A little love can overcome a lot of flakiness. Not that I think you're flaky. You've really made a great home for Nathan." He looked around the room at the scattered action figures, POGs, comic books and baseball cards.

"He picks up his toys before he goes to bed. Usually, anyway. Unless we get really busy doing something fun and bedtime sneaks up on us."

He grinned. "It looks fine. Like a real home. You can never be something you're not, Katie, and you shouldn't even try. What you are is pretty special."

His mouth clamped shut on the last word, and he blinked rapidly a couple of times, looking as if he had just realized what he'd said... as if he were as startled at saying it as she was at hearing it. She stared at him and he stared back, both frozen into place.

The back door slammed and Nathan charged into the room. "Aunt Katie, help me take off my wings. I gotta go to the bathroom."

With trembling fingers, Katie complied, and Nathan rushed out, leaving her once more alone with Travis.

"You are special," he said quietly.

"Thank you," she breathed around the tightness in her throat, and they stood for another awkward moment.

"Well, it was good to see you," he said, moving woodenly toward the front door.

"I'm glad you came by." Uttering the proprieties was the best she could do as she followed him, her head spinning so wildly she'd have been unable to protest having a root canal without novocaine.

He stopped at the door and turned back to face her. "I'm glad everything's working out so well for you, with Nathan, I mean."

"Yes," she said, "it is. Motherhood is my greatest adventure yet. Puts all the others to shame. In fact, I've decided to have a baby—a brother or sister for Nathan."

"What!" He stared at her in shock again, and she stared back the same way.

That was the first she'd heard about her new plans, but even so, she knew she meant it. She wanted another child.

"Who?" Travis finally choked out. She assumed he was asking her who the father would be, and she had another shocking revelation. She wanted it to be him. That was carrying this pretend marriage business a little too far. But there it was, flashing like a neon sign across her brain. She wanted Travis Rider in her life, wanted him to be the father of her children.

"I... I don't know." She turned away. "Maybe a sperm bank. Artificial insemination."

He grabbed her shoulders and whirled her back to face him, his eyes blazing. "You're lying to me, Katie Logan. You've done it often enough that I can tell. Is there another man in your life?"

"No. There's nobody in my life."

"Nobody? What about me? Am I nobody?" He paled and turned her loose. "Omigod, Katie. All these things I'm saying. I just realized something. This is no delusion. We're in love. I can't stand the thought of somebody else being with you, touching you, being the father of your children, growing old with you."

Heaven help them, he was as crazy as she was. She searched his eyes for truth and what she found there made her feel as though a sunbeam had just exploded inside her breast.

He slipped both arms around her waist and pulled her to him, his lips descending to hers, conveying their own truth. She lifted her face, her eyes closing as she allowed herself to greedily drink in the sensation of kissing him again. It had been so long! An eternity. Was it really possible she'd lived two months without being near him, without kissing him?

In the air-conditioned room, his body heat wrapped around her. Her skin tingled; she felt cocooned with him, the rest of the world a separate entity from the two of them. Her heart pounded against his chest, its rhythm perfectly matching his. She wrapped her arms around him, her fingertips exploring and reclaiming his back as her breasts pressed against his chest, her stomach against his, every touch a repossession. He was hers; she was his.

Time stopped. She was certain of it. If it were possible for a kiss to make her feel this way, certainly it was also possible for time to stop. She didn't know if it had been a minute or an hour when Travis lifted his mouth from hers and studied her intently.

"I think we're in big trouble, Katie. This feeling isn't going to go away. I love you. For real. Forever."

She lifted her hands to press against his chest, but lost control of them somewhere along the way. All they did was caress that chest she'd become so familiar with. She had a really scary, really exciting feeling that he was right.

"Say it, Katie. I need to hear you say it. I need to know I'm not alone out here."

She stared at him, her heart beating out an answer, her mind ordering her to deny that insane response. But her days of lying to Travis were over. She smiled slowly. "May God have mercy on you, Travis. I love you. But I'm not giving out any guarantees. I still might decide to move to a ranch in Wyoming. What would you do then?"

He studied her for a long, silent moment. She could feel her insides shriveling and suddenly realized how important this was to her. If he decided he couldn't live with her life-style, what would she do?

She pressed her fingers to his lips. "Don't answer that. Maybe I could give out a guarantee after all, just like I did with Nathan. Your love is more important than going off on a new adventure. It's more important than anything I can imagine."

"Then we won't be hearing any more nonsense about sperm banks. We'll get married the conventional way and have this baby the conventional way."

"Married? Are you sure? We've only known each other two days."

"No, we were married for two days. We've been together every day and every night for the past two months, haven't we? I know you've never been out of my life all that time."

His direct gaze challenged her to deny what she'd already admitted—dared her to pass up the chance to find him beside her when she turned to look for him, the chance to sleep next to him and give in to those impulses she'd had to fight in Oklahoma, the chance of a lifetime of the happiness she'd touched when they were together and pretending to be married. She might be a little flaky, but nobody had ever accused her of being stupid.

"When we were pretending to be married, that was the happiest time of my life. Well, except for a few worries like whether you were going to kill me when you found out the truth. The morning you walked out of the courtroom and out of my life, it felt as if you'd yanked my heart out. I've missed you so much. I don't ever want to lose you again."

"You never will, Katie. Remember when I told you it didn't matter how this marriage had started out? Well, just like you, I was telling the truth and didn't know it. All that matters is that we've found each other."

He lowered his lips to hers, and she responded with all her body and all her heart. This kiss was even sweeter than the others because she could look forward to lots more of the same. From now on, her life would be filled with kisses from Travis.

Before she totally lost her mind in the ecstasy of his embrace, she pulled away.

"I've been thinking about taking up race car driving," she said.

Travis's face scrunched as though he were swallowing something bitter. "Okay," he finally managed to say through gritted teeth.

She grinned. "Just testing. I've got all the excitement I'll ever need right here." She lifted her lips to his again and knew the adventure was just beginning!

* * * * *

HARLEQUIN®
Silhouette®